WHAT IF

Joseph Ingerson Mahar

J & S Mahar
patrobus@comcast.net
(856) 889-5718
maharjs.com

WHAT IF

JOSEPH INGERSON MAHAR

Imagine sitting at the table while your mother makes pancakes as she deftly plucks a fly out of the air and eats it. Or imagine you live a hermit-like existence making small animal figurines and your artistic creations begin to come to life. These are the kinds of inventive magical realism you will find in *What If* by author Joseph Ingerson Mahar.

What If is a collection of cleverly crafted short stories, each with its own unique fantastical spin. Although there are shades of Serling and Bradbury here, Mahar has his own style. One might draw allusions and metaphors from these stories, as is often the tendency in works of science fiction. And with Mahar being an entomologist, there is some science here. But overall, these stories feel like sudden flights of the imagination. The title of the collection perfectly sums it up: "what if" reality is suddenly interrupted by something fantastic?

The notion of "finding the extraordinary in the ordinary" is a common theme in this collection. "Looking Back" is a short, perfectly crafted story. It is quite simply about a man, Ethan, reflecting on his life after his daughter's graduation party. This story has the tone and eerie nostalgia of Ray Bradbury's short stories. It is short but quite poignant. "Benson Road Getaway" ventures more into science fiction. But again, it begins with an ordinary drive home and turns into an extraordinary encounter with a mysterious being. What makes the stories particularly engaging is the subtle way with which the author shifts from the ordinary to extraordinary. The author adds a note of magical realism wherein the characters are realistically reacting to the crazy "what ifs" that befall them.

This subtlety is noteworthy in "Morning Mad Mother," wherein the narrator wakes from a troubling dream into a reality that is just slightly off. Thus, it begs the question of whether he's awoken into an alternative universe or has slipped into another dream. "Morning Mad Mother" could also just be a story about the narrator's mother simply going mad. Ripe for interpretation.

There's not a bad story in this book, but I won't discuss them all. However, "Old Man in the Woods" needs to be mentioned because it could easily be an episode of *The Twilight Zone*. An old man, whose wife left him decades ago, lives like a hermit and spends his days making small animal figurines in his shop. The old man and his store function in a "limbo kind of existence." He has limited interaction with others, and lives by routine.

When a seemingly innocuous thing such as a woman asking for directions interrupts the old man's routine, a gradual butterfly effect occurs. When his figurines come to life, as magical as that is, the plot is driven by the fact that this man's routine has changed. Again, a seemingly ordinary thing made extraordinary. This change leads to other changes and the whole story, while firmly remaining in a twilight zone atmosphere, leads to the old man's life coming full circle.

I thoroughly enjoyed each story in *What If*. The author is quite adept at blurring the line between fantasy and reality in a way that makes the reader wonder if the events are actually occurring, metaphoric, or psychological tangents and dreams. The stories are page-turners: highly entertaining and thought-provoking: as all good science fiction and magical realism ought to be. If you're into these genres or just a great bit of escapism, give this collection a look.

Table of Contents

*To my wife and partner, Susan Ruth, for
forty-five years of marriage.*

Acknowledgement

To Dorothy Carpenter, my high school English teacher who urged her students to read and write creatively.

Thaddeus

The late afternoon sun shone brightly against the five- and six-story dilapidated city buildings across the street. They reflected the sun's brilliance in contrast to the ugly, brooding clouds that were moving in over them. The sky was rapidly filling with blackness, punctuated with flicks of distant lightning. The faint, booming thunder was coming closer and louder.

Arnold "Arnie" Wilcox stood next to the window in his upstairs apartment, brooding back at the clouds. With his prematurely thinning hair and stooped shoulders, Arnie looked much older than his thirty-two years. He stood there with his hands stuffed in his pockets, dimly thinking the coming storm fit his mood. He thought he might go out later, but the sky changed his mind. Besides, what was he going to do once outside? It wasn't like he was going to get a job or anything.

Arnie continued standing as the rain began falling. The wind picked up, and the lightning now licked the surrounding city. Instinctively, he edged back away from the window and into the dingy gloom of his sparse two-room apartment. The apartment building was old, and his frugal apartment was brown. There was no shade for the ceiling light, just a bare bulb that became more prominent as the sky darkened.

The storm now reached its full fury, with lightning lashing the rooftops and thunder reverberating through the building, shaking it to the core. Arnie pulled back further from the window and reached for a chair to sit down. As soon as he settled, the light bulb flashed out, pitching him into near-total darkness. For a few moments, he sat there as if soaking in the situation and then clenched his fist and smashed it into the table. Violently, Arnie snatched up, flung a wad of newspapers, and shoved the heavy table, skidding it a few feet. Muttering under his breath, Arnie made for the cupboard where he thought there might be another bulb.

The flickering lightning outside was a poor substitute for a flashlight. He groped around inside the shelves, tipping over various canned goods, and finally sat back. There was another light in the bedroom, a small reading lamp on the nightstand. Arnie felt his way into the bedroom, aided by lightning bolts, and returned to the kitchen/living room with the lamp in hand. Now, if he could only find the outlet. Another flash of light from outside outlined the outlet, and dim light filled the apartment in another moment.

After rummaging through his cupboards, Arnie was convinced he didn't have another bulb. It was too much for him. He slowly got back up from his kneeling position and slumped into the chair at the table. Laying his head down on his arms, he could feel the pressure building inside of him, of how desperate he had become. How pathetic he really was. Unable to hold his anger any longer, he let it out in gentle sobs at first and then a flood of tears.

Arnie hadn't always been like this. Not so long ago, he was near the pinnacle of his field. Mediocre in high school and unable to find a major in college, he eventually stumbled into something called finance and discovered he had a knack for numbers and taking risks.

Dropping out of college, he landed a low-paying job with a local financial firm and was on his way. Eager to learn, he progressed rapidly, changing jobs three times and landing with a major financial house. By the time he was twenty-six, Arnie was in command of his destiny. As he grew, though, his arrogance grew with him. He developed a reputation for being tough and ruthless. He became consumed with his work and had little time for socializing. When mandatory parties did occur, he wrapped them in work as he moved through the milling clients. There were rumors that his company was thinking of making him a full partner, but as time passed, the company owners became concerned about his astuteness and ruthless behavior.

When he met Brenda, he wasn't even thinking about dating. She attended one of the business socials and, afterward, found himself dating her rather frequently. Not that he minded. Despite dealing with his arrogance, she was attractive and seemed very interested in him. They shared common interests: music, cars, and finance. She seemed to enjoy looking over his shoulder as he waded through proposals, audits, and other financial papers. Within two months, she moved in with him.

They had become inseparable, even to the point that Brenda worked with him on briefs and began suggesting ideas on how to proceed with various projects. All of this was fine, and he marveled at how she had picked up on his work. Brenda had even suggested a plan to invest in his personal stocks and bonds. Yes, it was risky, but if the cards were played right, he (and she) would be set for life.

One day, near his thirtieth birthday, he came home to an unexpected sight. His penthouse was strangely empty. All of Brenda's things and some of his were gone. Not understanding what he saw, he checked his phone—no messages. He tried calling her number, but the recording came on and said that the number was no longer in service. He called his office to see if Brenda had left a message for him, and he was informed he had been fired.

In a rage, Arnie raced back to his office only to find that his keys didn't work. The security guards intercepted and let him into his old office to collect his few personal items, and two burly guards led him away. On the way to the front door, Arnie passed a custodian carrying a door nameplate with Brenda's name on it. Arnie was crushed.

After the initial shock, Arnie aggressively sought out other financial houses, but he had gained a reputation that soured most of the potential employers. He did land another job with a less-reputable business, but his arrogance soon had him looking through the unemployment sections of the newspaper. He tried headhunters, but they couldn't offer him what he wanted at the price he wanted. News came later that the risky venture Brenda had talked him into failed. She had bought his portfolios for pennies to show that her heart was in the right place.

The harder he looked, the more bitter he became until he realized he would have to start looking for other lines of work. He hadn't changed his lifestyle or spending and was so engrossed in his job hunting, he didn't realize he was rapidly going broke. Unable to reverse his fortunes, he had to move out of the penthouse and, after continual setbacks, eventually found himself in this goddamn, stinking hole! Nearly out of money and with no income meant he could stay in this dump for only another month or two, at best.

The crying spasm passed. Arnie raised himself up, changed his damp shirt, and headed out into the hallway. It was time to talk with the landlord. Harold Branson lived on the first floor along with his wife, Virginia.

Floorboards creaked as he made his way to Branson's door. From the fourth floor, he used the stairs. The elevator was hopelessly broken. It wasn't evident to Arnie what Branson spent rent money on. Chipped paint, cracked plaster, and worn carpeting adorned the hallways.

Presently, he came to Branson's door. Without hesitation, he began pounding on it.

"Hey, Branson. Open up," he said. "I need a light bulb."

He paused briefly, but there was no sound. Again, he pounded, and this time he heard a response.

"Open up, old man. I don't have all day, you know."

From behind the door, he heard a whiny, thin voice become clearer as it came toward the door. The locks were unlocked, and the door clicked as it opened a couple of inches. The only thing Arnie could see were black-rimmed glasses peering back at him, craning at an angle, indicating the owner didn't want to open the door further than necessary.

"I thought it was you. Well, what do you want, Mr. Wilcox?" The thin, raspy voice whined annoyingly.

"I said I need a light bulb."

"What do you think I am, a supply closet? Did it occur to you to buy one?"

"Look, you are the landlord. You are supposed to have these things. Now give me a goddamn light bulb, and I'll leave you alone."

Branson pulled back from the door with a scowl on his face. "You are not a nice man, Mr. Wilcox. You should develop some manners," he said sternly. He disappeared into the recesses of his apartment.

Slowly, the door swung open further. Arnie peered in. The interior of Branson's apartment appeared to be the same dingy brown as his apartment. Branson had moved out of sight to the right. Another voice picked up.

"Harold. Who is at the door?" The second voice was more delicate than Branson's yet just as annoying.

"It's that dreadful Mr. Wilcox, dear."

"Well, hurry and send him along."

As Arnie stood listening to the dialog, he caught sight of movement in the dimly lit apartment hallway. Something was moving along the floor. And then, just before Branson came back to the door, what appeared to be a broad, flat head raised from the floor and peered out at him.

A short, chunky man, balding with white hair remaining around the sides of his head, Branson came quickly up to the door blocking Arnie's view of the inner apartment. In his right hand, he held a light bulb.

"Here," he said, thrusting the bulb to Arnie. "It's the last one, so don't come back begging for more." A sneer curled up on Branson's face. "You know, Mr. Wilcox, you had better be careful, or I'll just have to raise your rent. Brash people like you deserve that sort of thing, don't you think? Goodbye, Mr. Wilcox, and be careful." Branson's pudgy face went from a pained expression to one of almost glee as he spoke. His last words faded into a threatening whining whispering.

The door slammed shut, leaving Arnie alone with a light bulb in hand. Strange old bastard, he thought, but Branson's last words unnerved him, and he hurriedly returned to his apartment. And what was that thing in Branson's apartment?

On his way back, Arnie recalled a brief conversation with another tenant shortly after he had moved in. She was an elderly lady who had lost her dog. She seemed quite worried and approached Arnie about whether he had seen it or not. Branson didn't like pets, and she was afraid that he had done something to it. He hadn't seen the dog, and come to think of it, he hadn't seen her since then either. Of course, it didn't matter to him. But now, he remembered Branson had warned him about having pets, so what was Branson doing with some kind of pet in his place? It was a puzzle that held no interest to Arnie, and he dropped it from his mind.

The storm continued to rage outside. Successive waves of storm squalls kept battering the city. Lightning flickered about the apartment like a strobe light in one of the local bars. Pulling a chair up under the light fixture, Arnie prepared to switch bulbs. Reaching up, he grasped the old bulb and twisted it, but the bulb was too tightly screwed in and broke in his hand. Startled, he nearly fell but caught his balance. A couple of the shards cut his skin. His hand was bleeding.

"Shit!" he snarled to himself. He climbed down and found some paper towels to stem the bleeding. That done, swearing at just about everybody Arnie could think of for his predicament, he located the fuse box to disable the circuit. He was going to have to remove the fixture to replace a stinking light bulb. Grabbing up a screwdriver from a drawer, he made for the heavy wooden table and shoved it out of the way. He repositioned the chair and once more attacked the fixture.

It was difficult to see the screws of the fixture in the gloom, and for several minutes, he struggled to take them out. The first one came out eventually. As he was trying to get the second one, a vicious lightning strike flickered, followed by a thunderous boom that shook the building. Startled, Arnie glanced at the window. Illuminated by the lightning was an enormous flat head peering toward him. A forked tongue flicked out, laying against the window. Transfixed for the moment, Arnie stared, mouth gaping. Another lightning strike, and Arnie lost his balance. Stepping backward, his right foot slipped off the chair. He fell backward, catching the sharp corner of the hardwood table in his spine just below his shoulders. His head, neck, and arms flung over the edge. There was a snap, and Arnie rolled off the table onto the floor. He landed on his left side, and his momentum put him flat on his back.

Groaning, Arnie roused. Immediately, he sensed something was wrong. He lay still, moving first his fingers. No pain. He could lift his head and no more. Pain throbbed in his back just below his shoulder blades, but from there on down, nothing. Coolly, he thought if he could pull himself into the corner, he maybe could prop himself up and call for help. Groping with his hands, he felt for the table legs, found one, and with all the strength he could muster, managed to pull himself a few inches closer to the corner of the room, but then the table moved instead. His weight was too heavy for the table to be an unmovable anchor. Exhausted, he laid his head against the floor and began yelling for help. The storm effectively covered his yells.

The head at the window continued staring into the apartment. The giant snake seemed oblivious to the storm and the rain pelting on its scaled body. After Arnie had fallen, the snake arched its head up further to get a better view. And after several long moments, the snake slid noiselessly away.

Arnie had no idea how long he had been yelling for help, but his voice was becoming hoarse, and his throat was dry. Finally, he stopped altogether. He wondered how long it would be before someone would check up on him. But then he realized that he had no friends, and his relatives had long ago disowned him. No one would expect him anywhere since he didn't have a job or set appointments. Ha, Branson would come looking for him to collect rent, except the rent wasn't due for another two weeks. How could he attract attention? He groped around with his hands again and found the screwdriver. His spirits immediately rose. He started jabbing at the floor with it, but it didn't make much noise, and as far as he knew, the apartment under him was vacant. A few jabs more, and he dropped the screwdriver.

Again, he tried to push himself into the corner where maybe he could at least raise his head against the wall. With titanic effort, using his shoulders and pushing with his hands, he managed to at least reach the corner, but he was exhausted. He had nothing left to try to prop his head up.

Miserable and frantic, he began shouting again. Between cries for help, he thought he heard a noise. A beam of light entered the room, cutting through the gloom. His apartment door was open. He could hear a soft scraping sound.

"Hello! Help! Is somebody there? I've fallen, and I'm hurt. Hello?"

There was no response.

He thought he must have left the door ajar when he returned with the bulb. The wind or change in air pressure must have eased the door open.

The large, flat head of the snake rose above his feet. Arnie couldn't make out what it was at first but shrieked when he realized what the head was. Arnie was staring at the largest snake he had ever seen. The snake's body lay in a pile between him and the door, about fifteen feet away. Its coils were massive.

He had no interest in pets, zoos, or wildlife beyond a bar and couldn't really appreciate this snake's size. But there was something about the snake that made him uncomfortable. He hurriedly tried to remember everything he had ever heard about snakes, which wasn't much. He was trying to hold his head up, but his neck muscles ached, and he had to lay back just long enough to rest them for a moment, and then he lifted his head again.

The snake's tongue licked in and out a few times, and the head shifted slowly to one side and then to the other. The snake pulled back. Hovering above his feet, the snake's head seemed to split open. The mouth moved oddly, and then the snake slid its mouth over his right foot with a slow, fluid motion.

Arnie flopped his head back. What? What was it doing? He raised his head again, and now the snake had slipped its jaws up to his ankle. The snake's body looped out beyond its head.

It suddenly occurred to Arnie that the snake was in the process of eating him! Stunned, Arnie couldn't comprehend this, but in his mind, he knew he was about to be the snake's supper. Arnie screamed louder than ever for help and thrashed about with his arms, but of course, no one came nor did his screaming seem to bother the snake. Frightened, Arnie looked up again to see the snake had now reached his knee. The snake was so large, his leg hardly made a bulge in the snake's body.

Arnie could feel slight tugs as the snake progressed up his leg. With a flash of insight, he thought this must have been what happened to the old lady who had quizzed him about her dog. This must be how Branson got rid of undesirable tenants. He mused on this for a moment, then snapped his head up again. His right leg was now entirely swallowed, and the snake's jaws were at his crotch. The snake seemed to hesitate.

"Now what, you stupid snake? You didn't think about how you were going to get that other leg, did ya? Ha!"

Arnie felt encouraged, but unfortunately, he had never watched a garter snake eat a frog. In dealing with difficult prey, the snake simply stretches its mouth wider.

He laid his head back. His heart was pounding, but he barely noticed. He called out again, but his mouth was dry and his voice weak. He closed his eyes, and when he reopened them, he saw his left leg rising slowly off to his left. His foot dangled limply from the knee. With aching slowness, his leg rose higher until the thigh was vertical. Arnie glanced at the snake's distorted head that was now slipping around under and over his butt. Though small, the backward-curved teeth of the snake were very effective in pulling the snake's jaws forward.

Slowly, his left leg began to fall back toward his chest. Arnie could see into the snake's mouth where there was a gap between his body and the snake. He reached down and touched the snake's head but was immediately repulsed. He forced himself to reach the snake and began to slap and hit at it, but he was too panic-stricken, and his blows were ineffective.

There was a call from the hallway. Someone was coming toward his apartment.

Arnie called out, "Help me! Help me!" His cries were strong, and he was sure that the person outside had heard him.

"Mr. Wilcox, are you all right?" The voice was high and raspy. A moment later, Harold Branson heaved his pudgy body through the doorway. Light flooded into the apartment, but it was bright, and Arnie couldn't see Branson's face.

"Thaddeus! There you are, you bad snake. I have been looking all over for you." Branson reached over, pulled up the chair Arnie had been standing on earlier, and sat down.

"Help me!"

"Oh no, I couldn't, Mr. Wilcox. I don't want to disturb Thaddeus when he is eating. For all of his size, Thaddeus is very shy, and any little thing will bother him."

It was true. The snake had stopped its consumption of Arnie. Arnie's leg was about halfway down to his chest.

Another voice called from the hallway. It was Virginia.

"There you are, you naughty snake. You had us worried sick, Thaddeus.

Shame on you," she cooed.

"Help me, please?" Arnie's request was faint. It was becoming increasingly difficult to breathe.

"Well, Mr. Wilcox, I believe this is the first time I have heard you say please. It will probably be the last time too," Branson chuckled.

Virginia moved her equally pudgy body close to Branson and looked lovingly down at the scene. "We are very proud of our Thaddeus, Mr. Wilcox. Don't you think he is just a marvelous snake?

Arnie couldn't understand what they were saying. Panic and hopelessness had nearly robbed him of his sanity. He could only turn his head and whisper, "Why?"

"Well, Mr. Wilcox," Branson's voice grew harsher. "You are a despicable person. You were rude to me when I rented this room to you, and you were rude to me today. Nobody likes a rude person like you. You are the same as any of those tenants who violate my rules, especially those who try to bring in pets. They don't remember my rule of 'no pets'! Thaddeus might have caught a disease from them. So they violate my rules, and Thaddeus gets a meal. But you are different."

He leaned over. "Mr. Wilcox, I *loathe* you," he said. "And so, Thaddeus gets another meal. Just think, Mr. Wilcox, in a few more minutes, and you'll be like a frog that a little snake catches. Squeak all you like; you'll be just a lump in his tummy."

"That's enough, dear," chimed in Virginia. "You know how Thaddeus hates to be interrupted while he is eating. He'll probably sulk for days now."

"Yes, you are right, dear."

With that, Branson stood up and, taking Virginia by the hand, left the apartment, closing the door tightly behind them. Once more, the room was in gloom.

Thaddeus wasted no time and returned to his task. Arnie's left knee came closer to his chin. Again, he reached down and slapped at the snake's head. He tried to dig at the scales on its neck, but the snake was unperturbed.

Now, it sped up its progress, having gotten past his hips. The edges of its mouth now reached his waist. The pressure of the snake forcing his leg against his chest made breathing more difficult than ever. Arnie knew the end was near. Hopeless, he flopped his arms out to the side. His mind raced through all the events of his life, and he couldn't believe he had come to this. He shook his head back and forth as he sobbed.

The snake's teeth reached the area of his body where he still had feelings. The small, sharp teeth immediately snapped his attention back to the present. The edge of the snake's mouth was near to his armpits. His left foot dangled out over his left shoulder. Arnie's broad shoulders were pushing the snake to its limit in stretching and slowed its progress. Dimly, Arnie knew that once past his shoulders, the snake would finish the job in seconds. He guessed he had maybe another minute at most before he would become the lump in the snake's stomach. How? How could this have happened?

Somewhere deep within him, Arnie felt deep hatred rising. All the wrongs of his life swelled together and drove straight to his resolve. With growing strength, he screamed out, "No!"

Again, he flailed his arms even as the snake's mouth was beginning to press against his shoulders. The snake's snout was a mere two inches from his chin. First, he pounded on the snake and tried to gouge its eyes. This made the snake flinch. Desperately, he groped around for anything that would help, and finally, he found the screwdriver again. Even as the snake's mouth was beginning to restrict his arm movements, he wielded the screwdriver in his right hand, stabbing it into its head again and again, again, again! Bits of skin and blood splattered about.

Thaddeus writhed violently and whipped its ponderous body around, trying to pin his arms, but more tightly than ever, Arnie managed to hold the screwdriver, screamed as loudly as he could, and stabbed at the beast a hundred times or more.

Finally, exhausted, his arm went limp. The screwdriver rolled out of his hand. It didn't matter. The giant snake lay still.

Dimly, he heard a noise in the hallway outside his door. Running feet.

Someone pounded on the door. "Open up, police!"

The door smashed open, with an officer standing there in the doorway with his gun drawn. He peered into the gloom, pulled out his flashlight, and panned the room. He saw the snake's body and followed it to its head and Arnie.

"Holy shit!" he gasped.

By the time the paramedics came, Arnie had passed out. It was a bit of a challenge removing him from the snake. It was not the typical sort of emergency they had been trained to do. Arnie came to several days later in a hospital. He had been in a pretty sorry state. Besides his back injury, the snake's digestive acids burned his lower leg and foot.

He was trussed up and couldn't move. The hospital staff told him of his spinal injury. They weren't certain how bad it was, but they were doing tests and scans. Would he recover? Too soon to know.

Time passed, and the healing process was slow. The back injury wasn't as bad as first thought, and there did seem to be a slight chance of recovery, and Arnie was determined to do so. Therapy introduced him to a wheelchair, so he learned to maneuver like an expert in time. The psyche would take longer, and therapy might last months, if not years, but Arnie was on the mend, physically and spiritually. A nurse named Angela from the hospital was helping to take care of him, to his delight.

The city museum was happy to claim Thaddeus's carcass. Despite the holes in the skin, the preparators felt a decent display could be made of it. Herpetologists from all over were anxious to see it because of its immense size. No one was sure what species it was as it seemed to be a sort of hybrid. DNA test results were pending.

Harold and Virginia Branson disappeared without a trace. When the police knocked on their apartment door, they found the apartment empty. A warrant for their arrest was issued, but they were never found.

Well-wishers and charitable organizations stepped in to make Arnie's life better than it had ever been. In exchange, he offered to help charitable organizations with their investments. Arnie had turned the page; his arrogance was gone. With the prospects of a new job and respect, he found a ground-floor apartment well suited to his needs.

Some seven months after the incident, Arnie wheeled into his apartment. He set a small sack of groceries that had been delivered on the kitchen table. After they were put away, he went to catch the evening edition of the news on television. Picking up the remote from the coffee table, he noticed a folded piece of paper.

Opening it, he found a hand-written note. His eyes widened as he read the note. The writing was thin and spidery:

Mr. Wilcox, I just want you to know that Thaddeus has a big brother. Sincerely, Harold Branson.

Benson Road Getaway

Morton Chase, an assistant professor at the university, pushed the accelerator hard as his SUV bolted from the feeder street onto the entrance ramp for the beltline. The Friday lunchtime traffic had swelled early, and the roadway was clogged.

"Pansy drivers, beware," he thought.

He was getting out of town as quickly as he could. Morton was a tall, athletic man in his fifties, but he handled the Explorer like a Nascar driver. Weaving and threading his way through the gaps of slug-like vehicles, he slowly inched his way along the expressway.

It had been a horrid week, and Morton wanted out of it as soon as possible. Everything that could have gone wrong did. On Monday, the department secretary had abruptly quit, leaving everyone in a lurch regarding purchase orders, account maintenance, and simply answering the phone. Her temporary replacement was horrible, having no idea what to do about anything except to answer the phone. On Wednesday, he had been notified that two grant proposals that were practically guaranteed to be funded were turned down. And to top it off, a student who had received a failing grade in his course had filed a sexual harassment charge against him just this morning. While no one believed the girl and his friends assured him that nothing would come of it, it was the sort of thing that would linger on, turning into gossipy stories about his escapades that would last for years.

He decided he had had enough. He packed his briefcase and fled the building. By 11:45, he was leaving campus, and now, at 11:57, he was caught in a traffic jam induced by road repair. The beltline traffic crept along, cramming three lanes into one. Morton chaffed at the stop-and-go traffic. His road rage quotient was rapidly increasing. Just before his breaking point, he managed to get past the road repair and was suddenly free. Every vehicle sped up to the normal traffic speed of 70 mph, and he was in the lead. Another reason why the roadways were clogged was the weather. An abnormally cold and wet spell had given way to bright warmth on this second weekend of June that spread over the countryside.

In a daring mood, he turned off the air conditioning and opened his window. The incoming breeze blew his graying hair around. For some reason, he had put on a tie this morning, but now he couldn't wait to rip it off. It was difficult to do one-handed, and finally, he pressed his knee against the bottom of the steering wheel and tugged and pulled on the tie with both hands until he had it wrenched off.

The interchange for the north-south freeway was coming up, and he prepared for the exit ramp. A stalled vehicle clogged the right-hand lane just before the ramp. Suddenly, traffic backed up. Uncharacteristically, he veered right onto the shoulder and slid past the slowed traffic, not caring whether any cops saw him or not. Spotting an opening, he gunned the Explorer and, amid a flurry of blaring horns, assumed his new position for exiting. Out on the freeway, he only needed to travel about 8 miles, and he would exit at last onto Benson Road.

Benson Road was a broad, well-paved road that flowed west into the distant horizon. Near the expressway, it was bordered by the usual assortment of truck stops and fast-food restaurants, but further from the exit, the landscape opened up. The road wedged itself through productive, well-managed farmland and out into the rest of the state. To the east, the roadway proceeded only for about two miles before the road's character changed dramatically. Blame it on the glaciers, he supposed, but there Benson Road became a narrow, twisting, pot-holed trail, leading drivers into a land marked by ponds and wetlands, scrub pine, and oak growing on sandy, low knolls interspersed with a few small farms. Eventually, it disappeared into a thicket of two-track dirt roads that led nowhere. It was toward the east that Morton headed. As soon as the tires hit Benson Road, he began feeling the tension ease in his shoulders.

Soon, he thought he would be pulling into the driveway of his secluded home, a rustic old house with unpainted woodwork and a magnificent stone fireplace. The fireplace was the envy of the department, and his place was especially popular during the fall holidays. He and his wife, Maggie, had moved here twelve years ago. They deliberately chose this remote, undeveloped wilderness to balance the madness and mayhem of the city. Maggie would be surprised, of course, to see him home so early, but she would understand and encourage him to talk about the problems at work, and eventually, they would be out in the garden or flower beds tending something important there before retiring into the house.

Maggie was a psychologist, though she never trained for it. She came by her skill naturally and would listen with focus when he needed to talk. Morton felt that attribute was Maggie's finest quality and loved her dearly for it.

Catching a glint of white tucked up under the passenger visor, he reached up to take down a copy of a plane ticket. Morton suddenly remembered that Maggie wouldn't be home. With all the aggravation at work, he had forgotten he had taken her to the airport early that morning to fly out to her sister's home. His sister-in-law had been ill for a while, and Maggie had decided to visit her. Morton had been so embroiled with the events of the day and week, he had forgotten that she would be gone over the weekend and maybe longer, depending upon how her sister was. He recalled her being worried about him and asked if he would be able to take care of himself. He snorted at the thought of her question. For Pete's sake, of course, he could!

But now she wouldn't be home when he arrived. No walk in the woods or gardening. The wine in front of the fireplace would be less joyful. Although it wasn't far now to the narrow part of Benson Road, he flattened the gas pedal and sped up. Within two minutes, he had to start slowing down because of the change in the road. It always struck him odd at how much difference there was in road repair and maintenance between the two local governments. Fergusson Township maintained Benson Road beautifully, but crossing the political boundary into Edward Township, the road immediately became pot-holed and decrepit. Of course, in Edward Township, there was a large natural area in the western part of the township where practically no one lived, so why maintain the road? The road condition didn't bother either Morton or Maggie, and in fact, they liked it that way to keep out new homesteaders.

Morton had negotiated the first mile of curving, cracked pavement when he caught sight of the white truck. Despite the curves and hills of the road, he soon caught up to it. It was an old white rusted delivery truck of medium size with a back door that slid up and down. The door wasn't latched, and with every bump and pothole, the door bounced and banged closed. The truck wandered over the road aimlessly as though driven by a drunkard.

Morton grew impatient. The ancient truck swerved and weaved about the road, straying across the near-invisible center line. Water splashed from the rain-filled potholes that it hadn't missed, forcing Morton to use his windshield wipers. He tried to pass, but the weaving of the truck, potholes, and curves made it impossible, so he continued following the plodding vehicle.

"Where is a cop when you need one," he snarled rhetorically.

He tried to make out the driver in the truck's side-view mirror, but it was cocked at an unusable angle. Road rage welling up again, he began blowing the horn, hoping he could force the driver to pull over or, at least, let him pass. But it made no difference, and the truck drove on.

Morton revved the engine to try to pass the truck when it swerved back to the right, but at the last instant, the truck sharply turned back left. Morton slammed on the brakes, bringing the Explorer to a skidding stop. Breathless, Morton laid hard on the horn until it reverberated through the woods.

Again, he pulled up behind the truck, determined to pass, even though his driveway wasn't much further. Morton began honking the horn, finally laying his hand hard on the center of the steering wheel. But the horn didn't faze the truck driver. The truck continued to lurch and weave, except a blue coil began looping, slipping out from under the back door. The cable drew out without touching the ground, and the end of it bobbed and weaved ever nearer to the Explorer. The cable tip swayed about over the hood of the SUV and finally stopped its movement when it came level with Morton's face. Morton, surprised by this action, couldn't help looking at it. He was both annoyed and perplexed at this thing but quickly saw that it wasn't a typical cable. It was smooth, steel blue, and comprised of three strands lying alongside each other, not twisted as in normal cables, and altogether maybe an inch in thickness.

Morton began to feel uncomfortable, as though the cable was eyeing him with an attitude, no less. He slowed the Explorer to a stop, and gradually, the cable pulled away, extending its length as the truck continued its wobbling course.

He resumed following the truck, now puzzled and wondered what the cable was, and followed at a prudent distance. The cable looped much of its length back into the truck, but the tip remained extended around the corner of the left rear of the truck as if it were watching the road ahead. It seemed oblivious to the bouncing of the back door upon it.

Suddenly there was a quick movement at the roadside at the edge of the weeds. A chipmunk lurched out into the road, deciding whether to beat the truck across the road or not. Instantly, the tip of the cable struck the chipmunk, with the cable strands peeling back, revealing long, slender needle-toothed jaws. Deftly, the jaws snapped up the chipmunk, flinging it into the air. The chipmunk sailed five or six feet up while the jaws opened up like an inverted umbrella underneath it. The jaws closed over the falling chipmunk, which quickly became a lump sliding down inside the length of the cable and disappeared into the truck.

"Shit!" Awe-struck, Morton gaped at what he had just seen.

He wasn't much of a naturalist, but he was certain what he had just seen was not a normal, ordinary event. Perspiration beaded up on his forehead as the cable once more resumed its lookout post at the rear of the truck.

So intent he was on the cable that he was barely aware of the back door of the truck sliding up. Like an electric shock, he jumped when he noticed the muscular, multi-hued arm reaching out from inside. The arm ended in a three-fingered hand with immense claws. It reached slowly and grasped the cable firmly. Instantly, the cable lashed and whipped around but was dragged back into the truck. Unnatural darkness veiled the truck's interior. Straining as much as possible, Morton couldn't see anything.

Moments later, the arm reappeared with the chipmunk in its claws. With a flick, the chipmunk sailed into the brush along the roadside. The arm then disappeared back into the truck.

Morton couldn't stand it any longer. He had no idea what was going on, but if there was a driver, he had to be warned about what was on the back of the truck. Frantically, Morton blew the horn and tried to come along beside the truck, but as always, the truck kept weaving about. Catching one of the potholes, the Explorer lurched right as the truck veered left. Only yards from his driveway, the bumper met a fender, shaking both vehicles and bringing them both to a stop.

Out of breath and shaking, Morton fumbled with the seat belt, trying to unhook it. Finally, he opened the door, but by the time he got his left foot on the ground, the cable had whipped out of the truck and menacingly came face to face with him. Suddenly, the cable strands peeled back, and those long, slender, needle-toothed jaws snapped at him, snipping off the very tip of Morton's large nose.

Yowling in pain, Morton grabbed the door handle and slammed the door shut. Blood dribbled from the end of his nose, quickly staining his shirt. Fumbling in the glove box, he frantically searched for a tissue and gobbed it up against his wound. When he glanced up, he saw the truck door had risen all the way up. Two of the large multi-hued arms extended out from the truck holding a large boxy contraption looking something like a tinker-toy construction with different-colored Styrofoam balls. An immensely wide but squat being thumped down to the ground holding the tinker toy apparatus. Morton noticed the head, or what he thought was the head, but there were no eyes or other distinguishing marks to suggest any human connection. Its body was covered in blotches of orange and green mingled with hues of gray and red. The short, thick legs rose atop large, splayed feet with no distinguishable toes. The being set the tinker toy softly to the ground and set about fussing with it.

The huge-clawed hands made some adjustments while the cable pulled back to the truck. Despite his injured nose, Morton sat transfixed. One clawed hand reached out and touched one of the blue balls. With a flicker, the ball turned bright orange, sending a bright orange line down the path of braces. Suddenly, with a zapping sound, a bright orange beam of light scorched the air between the truck and the Explorer. Morton followed the beam as it struck the roof of the car. With a slight puff, black dust wafted down onto his face from where the car's roof had been.

Horrified, Morton jolted into action, slammed the SUV into reverse, and gunned the engine. Before he could get away, the taloned hand touched a different ball, and a blue line traced its way through the construct. Nearly losing control of his vehicle, Morton had backed into the brush at the roadside and threw it into drive. Tires squealed, and smoke filled the wheel wells as a leaden blue beam fanned out across the road. A crackling sizzle sliced the air. Brush alongside the road made little popping noises, and some branches and leaves fell limply to the ground. A few birds cried out, and then all was quiet.

Mrs. Tompkins was returning home from a grocery trip. The back of the old farm pickup was filled with bags of food and supplies to last the next couple of weeks. It was getting late in the afternoon, and she hadn't started supper. Her husband and sons had been turning and baling hay all day and would be plenty hungry by supper. Driving Benson Road as fast as she could,

she didn't notice the wind gusting, nor did she notice the fine black dust on the pockmarked road whipping and swirling in the breeze. She did notice the old dingy white truck in front of her that strayed back and forth over the road. Mrs. Tompkins soon caught up with the truck. Impatient, she began blowing the old truck's horn. She noticed a steel blue cable looping out from under the bouncing back door that drew up to her windshield as though it was studying her. She slowed down to a stop as the truck stopped. She gaped in wonderment as some squatty figure brought out an odd tinker toy construction. Not comprehending what was happening, she sat there as a thin blue light sizzled through the air. Birds cried out, and a few leaves floated down amidst black dust to the ground, and all was quiet.

After the cable and the squat figure with its apparatus were back in the truck, the sliding door slid shut, and the rusty white truck continued its way down Benson Road.

Pardon Me

Normally, I arrive at the office around eight o'clock. I like to beat the rush, and it is always easier to find a parking place when you get ahead of the crowd. Actually, it's no big deal since we have a kind of a small office group, but even with fifteen souls, you sometimes have people eyeing "your" parking space. We had once tried to make an official parking space chart, but since people going to the Wawa next door sometimes parked in our lot, everything got scrambled, and we chucked the chart.

Anyway, this morning I am a little late. I walked in at about 8:18. Bad morning for traffic. That was one of the problems of living in a large metropolitan area like Philadelphia. Congestion, urban sprawl, and then there is the congestion. The phrase I had heard, learned years ago overseas, "Hurry up and wait," was very appropriate for describing even short commutes. A companion phrase, also picked up overseas, "Slow and steady wins the race," drags itself out of my mind occasionally, but I'm not a slow and steady kind of guy.

Despite my late arrival, I am still here ahead of nearly everyone else. Ted and Shelley are used to saying hi to me as they tramp in from the lot. Normally, I put the coffee on in the break room, and it's perking when they arrive—I always get the first cup. But today, I walk in and, well, what greets my nostrils but the aroma of freshly brewed coffee. But I can tell it's weak. I tossed my stuff into my office, snatched up my cup, and headed to the break room.

As I passed Shelley's desk, I said, "This better be good stuff."

"And what if it isn't?" she retorted. "Besides," she added, "probably nobody here knows how to make coffee anymore because you do it all the time." A pause. "Why are you late this morning? Accident or something?"

She gave me a slightly quizzical look, but her phone rang, and she let it ring twice before picking it up. She made a face as she brought the phone to her ear, indicating that it was much too early to be thinking about work even though the clock by now was inching toward 8:25.

I moved on to the break room and poured out a light brown cup of caffeine. And I was right—weak. Adding extra creamer didn't help, and after two sips poured out my cup, I dumped the rest of the pot and made a new one. Ted saw me dump it out.

"Good job. I don't think Shelley has made coffee in years." He made for the creamer, adding extra to his coffee.

He looked at me funny and said, "Hey, I'm not a purist. Besides, I need all the caffeine I can get." He glanced at me once more over the rim of his cup and turned out of the room back to his desk.

Involuntarily, I sighed. The wait for the new pot seemed to take forever. I leaned against the counter, hands in my pockets, and watched the rest of the office personnel stroll past on their way to their outposts. Perfunctory good mornings were murmured, and three or four of them were standing outside the break room waiting for their cups of java.

I glanced at the coffee maker, and the little red light came on. "Okay, it's ready," I pronounced.

I poured out my cup, dumped it in the creamer, and made my way past the rest lining up. *Hurry up and wait.*

I finally settled into my chair and proceeded to get to work. It was 8:37, and I was off my stride already.

I'm a paper pusher, like almost everyone else in the office. Only the two secretaries for twelve of us and one receptionist, a cozy little family who I didn't want to cozy up with today.

After a long-drawn-out sip, I reached for the first paper from the pile to my right and began to figure out where I had to push it. Several more papers came and went, and then I tackled the first file. By nine o'clock, I had successfully completed my second task of the day, and I felt ready to go home. 9:10 came and went, and I felt like I was stuck in tar or flypaper. The minutes began sticking to me. 9:11 crept onto the digital clock face and stayed there for an hour. I know this for a fact because I watched every second of it. 9:12 was even worse.

When 9:13 appeared, I shook my head, stood up, and walked over to my window. I have a great view out my window, cows in a pasture, and a small woodlot in the distance. A nice blending of city and country life for the moment, but this morning, I saw nothing at all.

Somehow, I managed to survive until 10:10, and then I headed back to the break room. Someone had made the obligatory run to the Wawa for our usual compliment of donuts. It's funny how we buy their donuts, but as an office, we seldom buy their coffee. I guess that's a testament to my skills.

I found myself sitting at the table with a half-eaten apple fritter in my hand. I couldn't remember picking it out or sitting down. Others began filtering in, and suddenly, there was a surge of the rest of the office piling in, grabbing for the best of the rest of the donuts. There are generally few surviving donuts by 11:00.

I saw a few people glance my way, but I didn't feel like acknowledging them. The table conversation began, and comments and questions and denials and other words floated and flowed around the room. One or two questions were directed my way, but when I didn't answer, more words directed at other people popped into the air.

A haze crossed over my eyes, and the scene of the intersection faded in. Sitting squarely in front of me was this rusted, ancient van waiting for its turn to make it onto the highway. The windows were dingy, and I couldn't make out details of what was inside. I recognized the vehicle for what it was: a van carrying migrant workers to the field this morning. I counted five heads appearing through the back window of the van, but previous encounters told me there were probably many more inside. They were on their way to one of the area vegetable fields to begin a day's work of doing something in the field. Harvesting, hoeing, I didn't know what.

Traffic was especially heavy this morning on 322, and the wait was long. The car in front of the van bolted out into the flow on 322 abruptly when the driver found a small gap between speeding vehicles. It always amazes me how the more congested the traffic, the faster it goes until either road construction or an accident puts the brakes on it.

The van ambled up to its take-off position. I had noticed when I first approached the van from behind that the rear tire on the driver's side was soft, nearly flat. I suppose the van was so loaded with men and tools that the driver may not have noticed any difference in how the van drove.

Traffic was so heavy that we sat there for what seemed an eternity. So long, in fact, that I realized I could have easily gotten out of my car and walked up to the van and spoke with the driver telling him about his tire, not once but maybe two or three times. My hand went to the door handle, but I didn't pull. Probably, he spoke Spanish and possibly wouldn't understand English. It would be a waste of time and frustrating for both of us. With my luck, there would probably be a gap just as I got to the van and the driver probably would have roared off.

I drew my hand back and sat there, thumping my fingers on the steering wheel, feeling ill at ease staring at that tire. I glanced quickly at the men inside, but I couldn't tell if they were eager to get into their work or if they were just trekking their way through what needed to be done. For a short moment, I wondered who these men were. What were their lives like? Did they have families, and if so, where were they, here or back home in Puerto Rico, Mexico, or wherever?

The van suddenly lurched as the driver was prepared to jump into a right turn but instantly hit the brake because he had lost the moment when he could have slid the van into oncoming traffic. The van rocked back and forth slightly.

At last, there was a sizeable gap, and the van's driver punched the accelerator, squealing the back tires. But it was too much for the soft tire, which burst, and as the van made its right-hand turn, it wobbled over the center line and was struck by a westbound semi. The van and its contents exploded.

I sat bolt upright and looked around the break room. Only Ted remained, and he was finishing reading an article in the paper. He looked up and said something about daydreaming and got up, tossing the now-folded paper onto the table. I really didn't hear what he said, and then I was alone in the room.

Somehow, the recounting of the accident made me feel better, and when I resumed my work, I was reasonably efficient. Lunchtime came and went, and I seemed okay, but then, at about 1:30, I began to drag, and once more, the feeling of being stuck in tar gripped me. But this time, I felt like I was sinking into it. I started to sweat, and I didn't feel well.

There was a bagel shop down a couple of doors, and I glanced around the office to see who might want to go down to the shop. I needed fresh air, and maybe a bagel would help me feel better, as well, but I didn't want to go alone. Right now, I needed company. Everyone seemed pretty engaged in their respective tasks. I glanced at Molly. She seemed very comfortable, and I started to head to her desk but then realized she was the receptionist, and she wouldn't leave her desk just at my request.

Shelley was the only other person that seemed to be a possibility. I took a deep breath and approached her desk. She was on the phone but hung up as I drew close. She didn't notice me at first until I spoke.

"Uh, Shelley. You want to go over to the bagel shop for a while?" I asked.

"We just had lunch. Besides, I'm sort of busy," she responded.

"Yeah, I know, but . . . well, I can't seem to concentrate and need to stretch my legs. Just thought you might like to come along. No problem if you don't." I stood there, hopefully, for a couple of moments and then started to turn away.

I guess she decided that something was bothering me and needed to talk with someone, or maybe I'm better at laying guilt trips than I thought. At any rate, before I had taken too many steps, she called after me, saying she was coming.

I held the office door for her, and she glided out into the foyer and then held the outer door for me. We walked in silence to the bagel shop. Once again, I held the door for her, drawing this response as she cocked her head to one side. "Something must be wrong with you today. You are being very gracious."

The early afternoon crowd had thinned. The bagel shop was popular, and there was always a crowd, keeping the place half-filled nearly all the time. We placed our orders and sought out a table. Again, we sat in silence, waiting expectantly for the call that our orders were ready.

I rose to get our stuff when the cook yelled out our number. Shelley didn't have much, just a half-bagel with cream cheese and a small Coke. I had a whole onion bagel with some ham and cheese, toasted. It was a habit to order that much. I wasn't hungry, but I felt the need to have more caffeine and went for a large Coke.

I returned to our table and set her stuff in front of her. She quietly thanked me and then, after another brief silence, said, "What's wrong? You have been acting like a zombie today. Did you have a fight with your wife?"

I glanced wryly at her and said, "No. No fight with my wife, thank you." I sighed.

Swiftly, the van at the intersection once again obscured my vision. The lurch, the slight rocking motion, the bursting tire, the collision . . .

The semi had hit the driver's side bumper, crumpling the corner of the van, and twisted it around so that it collided with the vehicle behind it. The van erupted, cracking open like a dark and rusted egg, spilling out brown bodies in jeans and long-sleeved shirts. Tools sprung into the air like straws mixing in with the aerial, sweeping movements of the bodies. The semi swerved to the right and churned into the road bank, taking out street signs and business signs. It breached the berm along the roadside and landed in a heap in the parking lot on the other side, smashing into more vehicles before it came to rest.

The car behind the van smashed into the side of the van, crushing the van as heavy groceries would do to a loaf of bread upon which they sat. The car-van mixture slammed into a utility pole, which snapped and leaned down over the intersection, drawing its lines and wires down with it.

As all this was happening, other vehicles squealed as their drivers hit the brakes, and several additional thuds were heard.

All of this occurred in slow motion, and I could see every fraction of each second of the passing time from start to finish. I saw the twisted faces of the men thrown from the van and the blood that was already spilling across faces, arms, and legs. The driver of the truck that had initially struck the van had raised his arms in front of his face as his truck plowed into the berm.

This horrific ballet cascaded to an end as bodies floated down and bounced on pavement and vehicles. Finally, the performance ended with everything being still and quiet. I don't know how many bodies lay still in the roadway, but they looked more like piles of dirty clothes waiting to be washed than like people, men lying in the street. There was no wind, no breeze. It was as if God had flipped a switch somewhere, and all motion stopped.

And then, I came to. Miraculously, there was an unobstructed path in front of me. I pulled my car out onto 322 and slowly drove around and between bodies and cars. Back away from the accident, people had already started getting out of their cars and looking at the carnage. A few saw me, and one large, burly man yelled angrily at me as I passed by on the shoulder of the road. In the distance, I could already hear sirens. I drove on to work.

A shudder has just snapped my attention. I look around and see that I am alone at the table. Shelley had left. I don't know when. The clock on the wall over a bulletin board in the bagel shop says 6:10, going on to 6:11. My cell phone showed that my wife had called not once but twice.

What's wrong with me?

Morning Mad Mother

Have you ever woken in the middle of the night for no apparent reason? Like you had a dream of some sort but can't recall a thing, yet here you are, wide awake in the middle of the night when you would much rather be asleep?

Well, that happened to me last night. It was pitch black. At first, I couldn't tell if my eyes were open or closed. I tried to calm myself by taking deep breaths and thinking about Amanda Stuart. After laying there for an eternity (Amanda hadn't helped), it struck me—something was in the air, a hunch. Something was wrong with the cosmos. I looked about but couldn't place my finger on it. Something was afoot—and close. Comforted by the fact that I had figured out what had woken me but agitated that I did not know what that something was, I dozed fitfully for the next several hours. Something was troubling the space-time continuum.

Morning came, and I trotted downstairs at the usual time and did the usual things: looking out the window to check on the weather, letting the dog out, letting the cat out, getting the paper, cursing the paper deliverer if the paper wasn't there, letting the dog in, letting the cat in (if she wanted to come in), feeding the dog, and finally feeding myself. Sometimes, this sequence deviated slightly so that I would feed Norm before getting the newspaper, but if Norm (the rabbit) didn't thump, I probably wouldn't remember, so it was his fault if I didn't give him any food or water. No thump from Norm today, so back into the house.

As I entered the back door, my heart started thumping like Norm's foot. The thing that had awakened me, that ripple in the fluid of the infinite cosmos, was revealed to me in the kitchen. This morning, mother had decided to make me breakfast! Why she felt so compelled was beyond me, but there she was, banging pans around, muttering to herself, her nightgown open one button too many. She was the sort of a mother who would look natural smoking a cigarette at 6:30 a.m. The fact that she never smoked didn't matter. Her face had the haggard, *"What the hell do you want?"* look that strongly suggested a cigarette should be dangling on the edge of her lip.

Her hair was a tangled mess—long, black, and gnarly. It sort of fit her mood. Morning sunlight had parted the clouds and was trying hard to squeeze in through one of the kitchen windows, but she had draped a hand towel haphazardly over it. A bright, cheery kitchen was a foreign idea to her. As I said, I had no clue why she wanted to make me breakfast. I'd have been much happier with her smoking in the living room, watching the morning news, and cursing at the TV.

I couldn't recall how old Mother was, somewhere between low, middle age, and ancient. But there she was in her nightgown, mussed hair, pink puffball slippers, her long skinny arms flailing about the space above the countertop as she rummaged through the cupboard looking for flour and other pancake ingredients. I felt a quiver of warm, fuzzy feelings.

"Get me the milk," she rasped. Damn, I wished that I had had a cigarette to stuff in her mouth. I gave her a wide berth as I made my way to the refrigerator. The 2% milk looked a bit sluggish to me, but when I hesitated, she snapped, "Hurry up!" I handed it to her, and while she grappled with it, I tried to slink out of the kitchen quietly.

"Hey, where are you going?" she demanded. "Sit down. I'm making pancakes, or whatever they call them." I dutifully took my seat at the kitchen table.

Flour poofed into the air as the bag slipped from her fingers, thumping hard on the counter. By the time the baking powder made it into the bowl, the counter looked like someone had murdered the flour bag with a knife. Instead of blood flowing across the surface, flour lay in piles and drifts. Yes, Mother had turned the fan on high, exclaiming that it was too hot. Had I had a camera for close-ups, I could have easily convinced someone with pictures that we had snow drifts in the kitchen. Global warming be damned!

Eggs cracked against the edge of the countertop with low-level cursing all the while. Pieces of eggshell fell into the developing batter. After several fruitless attempts to extract the eggshell pieces, first using a knife, then a fork, and lastly her finger, I distinctly heard an "Oh, what the hell." I knew I was in for crunchy pancakes.

A couple of houseflies had made it into the kitchen from outside. Their invasion of the kitchen probably happened while I was trying to get the cat to commit herself to either being inside or outside. I showed her no mercy when, almost immediately, upon shutting the door with the cat outside, the sky erupted with a sudden but brief downpour. Serves you right, I thought.

The flies were buzzing around. I didn't know that my mother had the talent of watching what she was doing with one eye while using the other eye for tracking the flies' movements. I thought only tropical chameleons were able to do this.

Suddenly, one of her skinny arms shot out, her hand snatching a fly in mid-air, popping it into her mouth. A toad couldn't have done it better. Forget the cigarettes. What I really needed was a cell phone. TikTok was calling my name!

For the first time in a very long time, I was totally enthralled with watching my mother. After popping the fly into her mouth, she continued as though it was perfectly normal to eat flies in the morning.

She grunted, looked about the kitchen, eyed me briefly, and then looked away. I breathed relief.

The second fly continued to buzz around, oblivious to the fate of its partner. It soon landed on the lip of the bowl of batter. With commanding, fluid motion, Mother flicked her finger, dumping the fly into the batter. Quickly, she stirred it in, then stopped. Apparently, my eyes were larger than normal. "What's the matter with you? You need protein, you know. Those kids in Asia and Africa eat bugs all the time," she exclaimed.

Now, as I sat mesmerized, Mother remembered she had forgotten to put sugar in the batter. I wasn't aware that cursing was an important ingredient in making pancakes, but apparently it was. As she stretched out her clawed hand, I was positive the bag of sugar was scrunching further back into the cupboard, but it was unsuccessful in its attempt to escape.

Triumphant, as mother poured in the last of the sugar, she bumped a glass of water onto the pan that she had melted margarine in. Water and grease fountained everywhere as a roaring hiss filled the kitchen. "Damn!" I heard through the mist. I should have made my escape at that point, but I knew she would only hunt me down, with or without the dog.

As the last of the vapors dissipated with the help of the fan, she managed to pour the batter into the pan. First, one pancake landed on a plate, then another, and finally a third.

Mother was always gimpy first thing in the morning. She listed like a drunken sailor as she shuffled her way to the kitchen table with my plate of three pancakes. Her movements were unsteady, as if the floor beneath her tilted with the tide. "Do you want any fuzzy orange juice?" she asked, her voice still scratchy from sleep.

I paused, unsure what she meant by "fuzzy." Was she referring to pulp? Or had the juice somehow fermented overnight? Not wanting to find out, I politely declined. She shrugged and plunked the plate down in front of me before bending to kiss my forehead.

Her lips hovered for a second, and then she froze, her face contorting in sudden horror. "God! Have you got head lice?" she demanded, her fingers diving into my hair.

I winced as her nails scraped my scalp, but I knew better than to argue. Denying would only make her more insistent. As her fingers dug around, I caught a glimpse of her out of the corner of my eye. Was it my imagination, or did she just stick her finger in her mouth?

"Hmm," she muttered after a moment, pulling back and squinting at me. "Oh, yeah," she finally said, as though something had clicked in her mind. She turned back to the cupboard, rummaging through its cluttered contents before pulling out a half-empty bottle of maple syrup.

"Nothing but the best," she said with a raspy chuckle, setting the bottle on the table. The label was long gone, leaving behind a sticky, mysterious surface. She hesitated, then added as she shuffled toward the living room, "If you find any hairs in the syrup, it's okay. It's just squirrel hair."

Squirrel hair? I stared at the bottle, momentarily reconsidering my breakfast choices. But hunger eventually won. As Mother stumped off into the living room to sink into her easy chair and absorb the morning news, I dug into my pancakes.

The syrup oozed down their fluffy sides, and I cautiously took my first bite. They were delicious—sweet and satisfying. Yet there was a crunch I couldn't quite place.

No hairs. No fuzz. And thankfully, I never did find the fly.

Looking Back

It was a beautiful, seasonably cool day with low humidity and plenty of sunshine. The turnout had been wonderful for Jen's graduation party, and now most of the relatives were leaving but several friends remained, and the party continued around the fire pit.

It had been difficult getting everything set up for the party, but they—he and his wife, Ellen—had done it. And now it was almost over. Ellen was still talking with one of her sisters in the house and, no doubt, was putting away some of the leftover food. Cousins and other family members had largely departed, and Ethan saw the opportunity to relax for a brief while. He pulled up a lawn chair, placing it in the shade of one of the backyard trees. Picking up a fresh bottle of beer, he slipped into the chair and gazed contentedly about the yard. Sitting there in the shade in the late afternoon, he contemplated all that had gone into the preparation of the yard and house and the food.

It was never easy when they had large family gatherings or other social events in the yard. Mowing the yard, washing the picnic table, adding tables and chairs, and generally cleaning the yard. Since the trees were always dropping twigs and sometimes larger branches, it was a near-constant struggle to keep the yard tidy.

Ellen tended the flower beds and was the major organizer for the party. Ethan usually waited for orders on what he was to do. But that was okay—he wasn't the sort of person to worry about planning too much. Hell, if it was left up to him, everyone would have to bring their own food, beverages, and anything else they wanted to have (nothing illegal, of course).

No, it was a good arrangement. Ellen was at the helm, and he did the leg work. It made life easier for both. With a sigh of relaxation, a gust of wind rustled the leaves above him. There was creaking of the branches, a crack, and a snap. Another branch was coming down.

Always the apple of his eye, both of his eyes, he thought. Jen had been precocious in most things: reading, reasoning, exploration, and just being inquisitive. She was always into things. When she was two and a half, she began dancing to music, even putting on a dancing dress and shoes. They had considered enrolling her in a dance school, but just about that time, Jen abruptly lost interest in dancing and started singing. She still twirled about while singing, but not with the enthusiasm she had shown at first.

At three and a half, Jen could really belt out nursery school songs. Later, she joined the youth choir at church. She continued singing to the present, joining college choir groups.

Jen had done it all: horses, 4-H, Mock Trial, student council, class president, charity work. Now, she was graduating from college with a BS in geology. Where and when did she develop an interest in rocks? Ethan shook his head in wonderment.

But Ethan felt remorse with Jen out of the house now for good. Jen was his only kid. He and Ellen had wanted more, but things just didn't work out that way. Nobody's fault. It was nature, chance, that dictated they would only have one child.

When Ellen and he had married, they were happy, but when Jen came along, they bonded even more. Ellen quit her job to stay home to care for Jen and recover. But the years of Jen growing up were the happiest they had ever been. Day trips, vacations, silly parties, summer picnics, winter snowboarding, and skiing, the three of them had fully enjoyed life. Ethan knew that he would be an empty nester, given the chance. He wasn't sure how Ellen would do.

Above Ethan, that gust of wind was all needed to finally snap a large weathered, dead branch out of the treetop he was sitting under. In the final seconds of his life, Ethan realizes that your life does flash by before you die, just as the branch crushed his chest.

Old Man in the Woods

The red Firebird convertible drove easily and smoothly along the twisting, newly black-topped road bordered by red maples, oaks, and jack pine. The fresh green color of mid-June vividly highlighted the northern Michigan landscape. Low humidity and cloudless sky made it a perfect day for driving. Long blond hair rippling in the wind, Alice abruptly slowed her convertible as she neared what appeared at first to be a gas station but was a general store. As she drew nearer, it looked abandoned, but then she saw a sign saying Open. Hoping for a bathroom and some directions, she parked her car near the front door. A faded yellow newspaper box holding a few copies of the *Detroit Free Press* stood beside the door. On the glass in the window was stenciled "Snacks inside."

It was hard to make out Alice's expression because of her oval sunglasses, but she was looking for adventure and just maybe she would find it here. Alice fluidly slid out of her car. Her long legs were coated with skin-tight jeans, and her long blond hair draped over her bare shoulders. Purposely, without hesitation, she strode to the door and entered another world.

Removing her sunglasses, she scanned the store's interior. As her gaze adjusted to the dim light, she realized that the store was ancient, with ancient dust. A few food items lined the shelves at the back. A pop machine with sliding doors on top hummed in one corner. On the shelf straight ahead of her against the wall were animal figurines: bear, deer, raccoons, and even a few trout were sitting there in ceramic beauty. Otherwise, the walls were bare except for a few faded, obviously out-of-date sale promotions. To the left of the door was a counter with a cash register, and behind that was a curtained doorway. Strains of Mozart drifted through the doorway. Though Alice despised classical music, she was now drawn to it.

Coming to the counter, she thumped her hand on it and yelled, "Hey! Is anyone here?" Nothing. Again, she called out. Just as she was about to turn to leave, she heard a response.

"Just a moment," a voice called back. Mozart's music abruptly ended, and seconds later, a figure appeared in the doorway.

Alice gazed at the old man who stood there. He was bald, hardly a hair on his head, and though he stooped slightly, he was broad and stocky. He wore a faded light blue smock with rolled-up sleeves. His trousers were faded and worn. Alice's gaze drifted back to his face, dominated by the hawkish nose. And then she noticed his eyes. They were bright blue and piercing, seeming out of place.

"Can I help you?" the old man asked in a firm voice.

Alice thought she detected an edge in his voice but felt a bit of a challenge here, and so, with a slight waggle of her rounded rear, she leaned forward with her elbows on the counter. Her low-cut blouse afforded the old man just the right view, she knew.

"Do you have a bathroom?"

Without hesitation, the old man said, "Sorry, broken." Taking a deep breath, she tried a different question.

"I'm lost," she replied innocently. "How do I get to Traverse City from here?"

"Just a moment," said the old man, who did not seem to react to her. He reached under the counter and pulled out a neatly folded map. Pulling it open and spreading it out, he pulled out his reading glasses and peered over the roads.

"Well," he said. "Go back down this road and, at the first intersection, which is Highway 68, turn."

There was a light shuffle, and the old man looked up. Alice had righted herself and stood there, arms crossed with a pouty, quizzical look.

The old man glanced up, and with understanding, he said simply, "Turn left as you leave the store."

Flashing a faint smile and a wave with her hand, she swiveled around, her hips pumped as she left the store. Convinced now that her adventure was waiting for her down the road, she didn't hesitate to leave. She knew she really hadn't given the old man a chance, but she doubted he was the right material for her. Soon, the Firebird glided out onto the road and was gone.

Inside the store, the old man stood there watching her leave. It had been quite a while since he had such a visitor. Alice would have been amused to know that the old man had taken in every inch of her and had already set a project in mind using her form, for he was an artist.

With a soft sigh, the old man turned and passed the curtain back into his studio. Though it was brighter here than in the store, it was unusually cluttered. Papers, wadded-up sketches, and various food containers littered the floor and any other flat surface available. After dialing up Mozart, he shuffled back to his sculpture and began to shape the clay again.

Minutes passed, and the lines of his work materialized, but vague impressions in his mind led to undesirable consequences. Sweat beaded on his brow while his face played out stressful expressions. The tension built up within, and finally, exasperated and seeking relief, he picked up the clay body. He hurled it with surprising strength against an already blotched and multi-hued wall. The deformed lump joined several other misshapen blobs already residing on the floor.

The old man slumped down on his bed, rubbing his large rough hands across his eyes and brow. His faint wisps of hair provided little to run his fingers through. With a sigh, he lowered himself onto the bed, ignoring the piles of paper that carpeted it. It was the girl's fault, of course. Damn her! She had broken his concentration, his mood. She had smashed his mind's image of what the clay should have been even more than he had smashed the sculpture. Of course, she was a beautiful girl, but that didn't give her the right to break his concentration. His head began throbbing like an emerging migraine. Exasperated, he downed some painkillers and fell into a fitful sleep.

When he rose, he saw it was dark, but that made little difference to him. He kept irregular hours, working on his art whenever he felt the urge, often in the wee hours. He seldom had an organized meal, just piecing as he felt hungry. The only routine he observed was on Tuesday mornings when he had a standing appointment at a local shop that served as an outlet for his commercial productions. Long ago, after his wife had left him, he realized the store wasn't going to provide enough money to support even his meager standard of living. As a result, he was forced into producing so-called "commercial" art, at which he was very good. In a rare moment of insight and planning, the old man had produced hundreds of figurines of North Woods artifacts: bears, ducks, loons, and other animals lining the shelves of a large cupboard. He had been observant of the wildlife in northern Michigan.

He showed rare skill in making the figurines in color and detail.

As for the store, well, that sort of persisted with little effort on his part. He never paid taxes and had even stopped thinking about them. His sales were so meager, he had stopped reporting any income. He would be hard-pressed to tell how the electricity stayed on if asked. The store operated in a limbo kind of existence. The delivery boy took care of the newspapers without addressing the old man. The soda vendor stopped coming once a week years ago and now only comes once a month or so. Occasionally, he noticed that the pop in the dispenser was nearly out. The machine didn't require money to operate. Patrons were on the honor system, and consequently, he really didn't make much money from it. But he didn't care. The store was a leftover from his previous life when he was young and married. Technically, he was still married, for he had never signed divorce papers. For that matter, he had never been given divorce papers, but when he thought about it, he knew he was as divorced as much as possible, if not legally.

In those years, he and his wife, in their late twenties, had moved to northern Michigan, looking for solitude to help them achieve their artistic desires. They had dreams of developing both the store and an outlet for their art, becoming a haven in the woods of sorts. In time, it was apparent that she was the practical-minded of the two, and it fell to her to make sure the bills were paid. Her artistic efforts suffered, and as time progressed, she came to resent her husband, who demanded that he not be cluttered with details of business.

A few more years, and she left. He was hardly aware she had left when he discovered a brief note. She did not say where she was going and that he shouldn't try finding her anyway. He didn't. Over the intervening years, he consoled himself with his work. He didn't require much human contact, and he got what he needed every Tuesday in the form of brief conversations with his buyers and a visit to a local restaurant.

But now, he was strangely restless. Alice had stirred up long-forgotten emotions and perhaps old guilt. Whatever it was, he couldn't work, and after several attempts to clear his mind with yoga and deep breathing, he resigned himself to bed.

The following day was much the same. All efforts resulted in frustrations. Even Mozart and Bach couldn't set his mind free. By lunchtime, he was frazzled. In a fit, he threw papers and anything he could lay his hands on. Chest heaving, he scowled at the mess around him. Beads of sweat formed on his forehead from his exertions. Savagely, he yanked a dirty towel out from under one of the floor piles and stormed out the back door of the studio.

A path from the back of the building led across a scraggly narrow yard on into the woods behind. The old man followed the path into the coolness of a red maple/oak/pine forest until he came upon a stream. The path turned and followed the stream to a pond that had backed up behind a beaver dam. At one low open edge of the pond, he pulled off his shoes, rolled up his pant legs, and stepped into the cold water. The chill crept up his legs as he strode out into the water. The pond was shallow, no more than three or four feet deep in the deepest part.

The coolness seemed to dissipate the pent-up energy in his body. He began stepping higher, splashing the water a little, then slapped the surface with his hand. He began to giggle. Soon, he was smacking and splashing the water, cavorting around like a small child. His laughter resounded amongst the trees and greenery around the pond. He felt invigorated, and the better he felt, the more vigorous he became. Now drenched, he slipped in the bottom ooze and fell backward. He didn't try to catch himself but let his weight pull him down into the water. Submerged on his back, he spread out his hands, swam underwater for a short distance, and then exploded out of the water, only to fall back in again. Out of breath and laughing deeply, the old man rolled over to his knees and began crawling to the pond bank.

His hand penetrated the ooze to the underlying clay a few feet from the edge. At first, he thought he had pricked himself on something sharp, for he felt an odd jolt on one of his fingers that sent a tingle up his arm. He sat back in the water and pulled his hand up to his face. He saw nothing protruding from his finger nor a wound of any sort. Wondering, he tentatively pushed his fingers back into the ooze. He touched the clay, and again, there was a sharp tingling that shot up his arm. He pulled his fingers back and then stuck out his first finger and touched the clay once more. His finger tingled as before.

Mystified, the old man reached through the layer of ooze and scooped out some of the clay. Sitting down in the water, he brought it up to his eyes for closer scrutiny. It was silver streaked with brown, had a very smooth feel, and was very malleable. As he worked the clay in his hands, the tingling coursed through both hands and up his arms. Never had he ever felt anything like this before.

Looking around, he found a broken tree branch and used it to mark the spot where he had found the clay. Then, sopping wet, he hurriedly slipped his shoes back on and half walked, half ran back to the studio. Rummaging through the trash, he found a bucket and a trowel from amongst his meager tools and returned to the beaver pond. Carefully now, he entered the water, setting the bucket on the bank. With the trowel, he scooped up as much clay as he could and then deposited it in the bucket. It wasn't long before his bucket was full. He stepped out of the water, shoes squishing. Coming back to the pond, he was so excited that he hadn't bothered taking his shoes off. Even though the air was warm, he began shivering, but it was as much from excitement as from being chilled from the water. The bucket was heavy, and after carrying it a few yards, he had to switch hands. The water in his shoes squeezed around his toes as he walked. When he reached his studio, he was quite out of breath for it was a large bucket and held maybe eighty pounds of clay.

The old man stripped off his clothes, dried himself off, and donned dry, wrinkled clothes. He then went back to the clay and pressed his hand into the bucket to make sure the tingling was a real sensation. As he touched the clay, his hand nearly vibrated with the tingling. He dug out a large chunk of the slippery, wet clay and molded it in his hands. The tingling spread through his hands and up his arms. The longer he held on to the clay, the more the tingling turned to warm his hands and arms. His shoulders felt tense but warm. He laughed again at the marvel of the clay, and he set about sculpting it.

He quickly formed several different figurines. He put three of them inside the kiln, turned it on, and looked expectantly at it. He wasn't sure that he could endure the wait until the following day to see how they turned out. For the rest of the day, overnight and the next morning, the old man was impatient. Several times, he went to the bucket of clay to assure himself of what he had felt by touching the clay. He had covered the bucket to keep the clay surface damp. Otherwise, he fiddled aimlessly about the studio and store. Needing to occupy himself, he set about trying to pick up the mess around the studio, soon realized it was hopeless, and dumped everything that he had picked up in a pile in one of the corners. He found a lone box of crackers in the cupboard that the mice hadn't gotten to and munched away on those.

Sleep was impossible. He was so restless. The excitement of the new clay was too much. But finally, exhausted, he dozed off. The next morning,

he woke up late when someone came into the store. "Just getting a pop," a voice called out. "Help yourself," the old man responded. The voice sounded like one of the locals.

Finally, the kiln had cooled so that he could take out the figurines. Opening the top of the kiln, the figurines looked okay. Carefully lifting them out, he set them on the countertop. As the figurines sat there, he noticed small cracks were appearing here and there. The longer he watched, the more cracks appeared, and the figurines began to crumble. Within an hour, they had all crumbled into piles of clay dust. He touched the piles. There was no tingling, just dust that blew away. Startled by this development, he added water to the dust but only got a thick paste. Whatever property the clay had before firing it was now gone.

What was wrong? What could he do? Finally, with patience running out, he picked up one of the unfired figurines and threw it, and then another. There were a few sitting next to the sink, and with a backward sweep of his arm, he knocked them into the standing water of the sink. In that sweeping motion, he also knocked the cassette player into the sink, which had been playing soft classical music the whole time.

There was a loud *phfzzt* and a puff of steam that startled him. Realizing what had happened, he quickly grabbed up a broom handle and knocked the plug out of the wall outlet. Breathing deeply, he turned to survey the scene when he heard peculiar noises coming from the sink. Cautiously, he peered over the edge and gaped at what he saw. A miniature bear, a wolf, and a mallard duck were struggling in the water. His mind reeling, he stood there motionless. Yes, these were some of the figurines he had made. He hadn't painted them, just formed them and planned to fire them in his kiln. But here they were, wet, in the sink, with all the color and markings the real creatures would have.

Standing there, he couldn't understand what had happened. He wanted to move, to look at them more closely, but he was firmly anchored to the floor with fear and wonderment. After what seemed an eternity, the animals calmed down and began to look at him. The bear and wolf with wet fur stood chest-deep in the water, watching him. The duck had swum about the sink, but now, as it circled about, it kept looking up at him. Carefully, he lifted the tape player out of the water and set it aside.

Slowly, he stretched out his hand to the black bear, bringing his fingertips to the tip of the bear's nose. The bear acted agitated at first but then began sniffing his fingers like a dog might. With great care, the old man reached around the bear, picked it up out of the water, and held it in front of his face. The bear was calm and allowed himself to be held without fuss. The bear even let the old man roll him over so he could see every inch of its body. The old man set the bear back in the sink but then thought he should let the water out of the sink. The wolf shook himself as dogs do when wet, but the duck squawked louder as the water disappeared down the drain.

The three animals milled about in the sink, making soft growls, barks, and squawks, but kept their gaze on the old man. He was perplexed. What was going on here? The animals were acting as though they were waiting, expecting something from him. For several long minutes, the old man just stood there trying to make sense of it all. Their noises gradually became louder, and their actions became more agitated. The bear and wolf began to snap at each other, while the mallard squawked louder and avoided the others. Suddenly, the mallard flapped its diminutive wings and took a flight out of the sink, startling the wolf and bear. The old man let out a woof of air as he stepped back to watch the mallard fly up around the ceiling. After a minute, it flew down and landed on the edge of the sink. Momentarily distracted, the bear and wolf continued growling and snapping at each other.

With sudden insight, the old man hurried off to the refrigerator and pulled out a half-used packet of sliced pepperoni. Taking the package back to the sink, he pulled off a couple of slices and dropped them into the sink. Glancing up at the old man, the predators approached the pepperoni and sniffed at it. The bear pawed at one piece and then licked it before it ripped the slice apart. The wolf watched the bear, hesitantly sniffed the other slice, and then gingerly began nipping at it. In a couple of minutes, the bear had pretty much devoured its piece, but the wolf still had half a slice and convinced the bear it should leave the slice remnants alone.

In the meantime, the duck wandered about the edge of the sink keeping a watch on the old man but also looking at the furry animals in the sink. The old man looked at the bird and then searched for an old box of bird seed he used to attract birds to a window box feeder. Finding it, he brought the box of seeds over and poured out a little onto the counter next to the sink. The mallard waddled over to the birdseed, nosed it around, but did not eat any of it. The mallard began to protest even louder.

The old man found some stale bread, soaked a little of it in water, and laid it before the duck. After a moment of hesitation, the duck nibbled up all the bread lying there. His feeding chores ended, the old man staggered back, found a chair, and sat down facing the counter and sink. All three of the animals stared back at him as though waiting for something. He stood and roamed about his room, his mind bursting with ideas, concerns, and what-ifs. He finally stopped beside his bed and lay down. Soon, he dozed off, and though he didn't know, the three clay animals dozed off as well.

The sky was overcast when he woke up, and an early morning storm seemed likely. It was quiet in the workshop. As he rose from the bed, the mallard also stirred and watched him move about, soon from the sink. The bear and wolf were moving about and, from the sounds of it, didn't like being penned in the sink.

The old man leaned over the sink, carefully lifting the bear out of the sink and setting it on the counter. The bear grunted and looked over its new surroundings. Next, the old man reached for the wolf. It was skittish at first but allowed him to close his fingers around its body and lift it out onto the counter as well.

Feeling hungry, the old man searched for food, and while at it, he pulled out another couple of pieces of pepperoni and some more bread. He dropped these on the counter in front of the animals, and they all began to eat. He rummaged through the cabinets, finding a box of flake cereal. He poured some into a bowl and, lacking milk, added a little water before scooping it into his mouth.

The three animals seemed satisfied. After preening and licking their coats, they sat and stared at him. A thought had occurred to him during the night, and now he made his way to the bucket of clay. He stuck his finger into it and felt the familiar tingling. Raising his brows, he turned and bent over to touch the half-formed, crumpled pieces of clay on the floor. Nothing. The unfired figurines were just dead clay. As he touched them, they began to crumble, turning into powder. Wetting the powder, it remained nothing but wet.

Trying to think logically, he reasoned that he had once sculpted live animals after they were electrocuted in the sink. So he should recreate the conditions that had brought the original three to life. He took out more clay and sculpted another bear. Carefully, he placed the bear into the sink and filled it with water. Being made of clay, the figurine stayed intact. The next question was: how was he going to provide the electricity? The little cassette player was no longer an option. What else could he use?

Rummaging through the kitchen, he found an old electric can opener. He plugged it in—and it worked. Quickly, he took it to the sink but hesitated. The can opener was larger than the cassette player, and only one creature was in the sink. This didn't feel right.

He went to the pile of tools in a distant cabinet, grabbed pliers, and first cut the cord of the can opener. Then, he stripped the two wires of their plastic coating. Turning back to the sink, he plugged in the cord and dropped the exposed wires into the water. He had left his left hand resting on the edge of the metal sink, forgetting its conductivity. As soon as the wires hit the water, a jolt of electricity zapped his hand, flinging him back and slapping the cord out of the sink in the process.

Stunned, he rubbed his hand and arm, slowly making his way back to the sink. Peering in, he saw another bear, fully colored and as real as life. It was swimming in the water, but like the first animals, it locked its gaze on him and followed his every move. Delighted, he slowly reached in, lifted the bear from the water, and set it on the counter. This time, he didn't hesitate. He found the packet of pepperoni and offered a slice. The bear sniffed the meat, much like the first one had, then proceeded to tear it apart.

The old man staggered back, clumsily sitting down on his bed. Now, there was a bear on the edge of the sink, one more on the floor, along with a wolf and a mallard duck flying overhead. He stared at the new animals, giggling at first, then growing more giddy as he broke into a broad smile. His four animals seemed to reflect his mood, frolicking in their own ways.

His mind raced, and in short order, he created another five animals: another bear, two wolves, a fox, and another mallard. His menagerie was growing faster than he expected. But as the excitement faded, concern crept in. How was he going to feed all these animals? He had only a few bits of pepperoni left. The ducks wouldn't be a problem, but the other predators needed meat. Luckily, his sloppy eating habits had left plenty of food scraps scattered on the floor and stuck to papers and wrappers. The bears, wolves, and lone foxes were helping by searching out the tidbits and eating them, even chasing after the insects attracted to the scraps.

The figurines he made for the shop in town were small— usually four to five inches in length, regardless of the species. But his ducks were as large as the bears, elk, and deer. He had entire shelves devoted to his figurines and likely would never run out.

But this new clay was amazing. He didn't need to focus on all the details as he usually did with his regular work. All he had to do for the new clay animals was outline the species, and after the electric shock—voilà! A new bear, duck, fox, or whatever he had in mind came to life. The clay seemed to know exactly what he envisioned as he sculpted.

Over the next couple of days, he worked feverishly, creating new animals of various species: elk, deer, squirrels, and geese. He briefly considered sculpting fish but quickly dismissed the idea. Too messy, too much work.

On Tuesday, he went into town and sold more of his usual commercial art. His figurines sold out quickly, and the shop owner was always eager to place new orders. The old man had long ago decided not to sell from his own store—it would be too much of a distraction, and besides, even he needed to see the outside world now and then. But the joy he found in creating his living creatures was so great that he decided to skip his usual Tuesday ritual and instead focus on the following Tuesday.

Though it wasn't exactly a problem, he wondered if he should try selling some of his living animals. Somehow, though, it didn't seem right. He was getting such a rush from bringing them to life—more than he could have ever imagined. His artwork was coming alive. One thing he had wondered about was whether the predators would try to eat the herbivores, but that hadn't happened. The bears, in particular, were excellent at foraging through the piles of trash around the studio, doing a superb job of cleaning up food scraps and crumbs. Using their pack instincts, the wolves developed a knack for tracking down mice. The foxes, about the same size as the wolves, worked alongside them but also struck out on their own, hunting insects and other small creatures.

Early Tuesday morning, he brought out a box full of his commercial figurines and set them on the back step. Years ago, he had renovated a large trunk that now sat in the back of his 1986 Chevy S-10 pickup. The trunk had three partitioned shelves, creating 144 cells—each just big enough for one figurine. The truck was housed in a dilapidated garage that barely kept out the rain and snow. Despite its age and neglect, the truck looked decent and ran well. Opening the garage doors took some effort, as weeds had grown up around them. Going to town once a week wasn't enough to keep them at bay.

He dressed carefully for the trip into town—shaving, putting on a clean smock, and donning a rumpled wide-brimmed hat. He noticed that his live animals seemed distracted, milling about aimlessly as though they knew he was about to leave. By now, he had an army of bears, wolves, foxes, bobcats, squirrels, beavers, elk, deer, and a couple of moose. There were also several geese and ducks, which required more trips to the beaver pond. He'd lost track of how many he had created, but he had developed a real production line for making more. His biggest concern was running out of food for his predators, so a grocery store stop was mandatory.

Now that he was ready to leave, he felt a reluctance to go. He glanced at his creatures gathered near the back door, and with a sense of unease, he carefully edged his way out, making sure to close the door without crushing any of them.

It was a twenty-minute drive to Baldwin, where there was a sports shop that bought his figurines. Jimmie Samson owned the shop. It did brisk business during hunting season but was a bit off the beaten path for tourists in the summer. Still, Jimmie always bought the old man's carvings, and nearly every customer left the store with at least one.

The old man pulled up in front of Jimmie's Hunting and Fishing Shack, parking near the back door. With some effort, he got out of his pickup and made his way up the two steps into the store's backroom. Jimmie had told him to use the back door, where tables were set up for him to display his figurines, right next to the cooler filled with worms and nightcrawlers.

Going through an open doorway, he entered the main part of the store, where hunting and fishing equipment lined the walls. Live bait was stocked at the back, and souvenirs and snacks were scattered wherever there was room.

"Hey, there he is!" Jimmie called out as the old man emerged from the back room. Jimmie, a rough-around-the-edges sixty-year-old wearing glasses, a battered Tigers baseball cap, a plaid shirt, and suspenders, was standing behind the cash register. A display rack of hooks and lead weights stood next to him.

"I was starting to worry you got run over by a timber truck or something," Jimmie joked. "There's a back road not far from here where a truck broke a bridge. They never replaced it—just a sign saying, 'Bridge Out.'"

"Hi, Jimmie," the old man grunted. "How many do you want? I'm raising the price. Food's getting expensive."

"Hey, I can't pay too much for them. If I raise my prices, nobody's gonna want to buy them."

"Horse shit! Three dollars each," the old man countered. "How many?"

"Uh, you got fifty of them? The geese and ducks sell the best. You really bring them to life."

At that, the old man, peering out from under the brim of his hat, glanced up at Jimmie and faintly smiled.

"Okay, maybe you should give me seventy of them. You got seventy? Mix 'em up, but make sure you give me a bunch of the birds. The Fourth of July is coming up. They'll be good sellers."

The old man turned back to his truck, loading twenty figurines into a box, making four trips back and forth. He had carefully wrapped each one in newspaper, pulling them out one by one. Soon, seventy animals in various poses were spread across the table: thirty-two birds and the rest a mix of bears, wolves, foxes, deer, elk, and moose.

Jimmie entered the back room and surveyed the array.

"They look great. You always surprise me with how lifelike you make them." Noticing the old man looked tired, he added, "You know, if you had a cell phone, you could just call me, and I could tell you how many to bring in. It'd save you time and effort."

Just then, the tinkle of the front door opening caught Jimmie's attention. "Oops, customer. Here's your dough—$210."

The old man tentatively reached out for the envelope.

"Hey, don't worry. It's all there. You know I wouldn't cheat you. See ya."

Jimmie disappeared, and the old man grabbed his box. He briefly stepped

into the store, where Jimmie was talking about fly fishing with a father and son. The old man gave a slight wave, and Jimmie nodded in response. Back outside, he loaded the box into his truck, drove up the highway to buy groceries for himself and his newly formed animals, and then on to Johnny's Log Bar.

At the grocery store, he scanned the shelves, searching for food not only for himself but for his animals, especially the predators. After some thought, he decided on canned chicken. He bought several cans, adding fresh fruit for himself, a loaf of wheat bread, and other snack foods. He didn't need to buy anything for the deer, elk, and moose—pulling grass and weeds seemed to work just fine for them. Surprised by the high cost of his groceries—nearly a hundred dollars—he hefted two bags and made his way to his truck. After loading everything up, he pulled out of the parking lot and headed to Johnny's.

There, he parked, locked the truck, and entered the bar. It was hot and bright outside but cool and dark inside. If there was a vacant spot, he would always sit next to the bay window, looking out onto the street. From there, he could observe the people on the sidewalks, noting their differences: height, weight, hair color, skin tone, and any other notable features. It was, for him, like getting a new catalog of products.

Just his luck—his favorite booth was free. Without hesitation, he made a beeline for it, slid into the seat, and officially claimed it as his own. He set his hat at the window end of the table and scanned the view. There were a few people moving about, but before he could become too distracted, a voice snapped him back to the present.

"Hey, my favorite artist. How's it going?"

It was Shayna, a black woman in her fifties, his favorite waitress—actually, his only waitress. The old man had been coming in for years, and from the beginning, Shayna had been the only one he wanted waiting on him. They had a bond that felt good, and besides bringing in his artwork, he looked forward to his meals here with Shayna.

"You didn't come in last week. What happened?"

"I was busy. Got a new project." "Tell me about it."

"I can't. It's special." The old man squirmed in his seat, suddenly feeling a little agitated. He hadn't expected to be questioned, and it made him uneasy.

"How about food?" he changed the subject.

"Yessir, coming right up." Shayna poured a glass of water, patted him on the shoulder, and returned to the kitchen.

The old man turned his gaze back to the people outside. There weren't many this morning, but more would appear as the day wore on. The ice cream shop at the other end of Main Street always did phenomenal business and would draw in the crowd as the temperature rose.

After a few minutes, Shayna returned with his food. He inspected it to make sure everything was in order: a Western omelet, wheat toast, a hamburger, and a dish of applesauce.

"I'll bring the Guinness in a minute," she said.

The old man gave a thumbs-up and began eating his omelet. After a few bites, he lifted the omelet with his fork. A burnt match lay there on the plate. Smiling, he placed the omelet back down and turned to beam a smile at Shayna, who smiled back.

When he had first started coming to town to sell his figurines, he had stopped at what was then the 7th Street Grill. He'd ordered a hot beef sandwich, and as he ate, he found a burnt match hidden under the sandwich. He didn't know whether it was intentional or a mistake, but either way, he decided not to go back there. After he started coming to Johnny's Log Bar, he told Shayna about the match. She was aghast that anyone would leave a burnt match on a plate of food. It would never happen at Johnnie's, she assured him. Naturally, the next time he came in for a meal, there was the burnt match.

Shayna apologized but explained she wanted to make him feel at home, so she'd kept the match tradition going. Since then, it had become a running joke every time he came in. It made him feel special.

Shayna brought his Guinness toward the end of his meal. Now, the old man would sit quietly for a time, sipping it before getting up to leave. But suddenly, he snapped back into focus. His animals were waiting back at the studio. He had gotten them food, but they still needed to be fed. Guzzling the remainder of his drink, he got up and headed for the cash register. As he handed Shayna his money, he briefly laid his hand on hers, smiled, and left. Shayna gave a little wave as he went out the door.

The drive back home was uneventful. When he got there, he hurried through the back door into the studio and glanced around. As far as he could tell, all the animals were looking at him. The more athletic animals and the birds were on the tables and countertops, while the predators were mostly on the floor among the moose, deer, and elk. He quickly opened the canned goods and set them on the floor. Immediately, the predators gathered, snapping up bits of chicken. For the birds, he laid out breadcrumbs for the geese and ducks, but he also had two bald eagles, which he gave chunks of chicken. Lastly, for the deer, elk, and moose, he went outside to collect grass and leaves from several different plants and laid them on the floor. The herbivores were the pickiest, and he decided not to create more of them.

The next several days passed with the old man enjoying his menagerie. He became convinced that his animals displayed the same emotions he felt. When he was sleepy, the animals would act tired and lie down. If he was excited, they'd show the same. If he threw another lump of clay at the wall, the animals would growl, bark, or hiss at each other. He decided that he had enough animals now. The novelty of creating more was wearing off. Besides, he was having trouble moving around the studio, afraid he would step on one. And then there was the scat—the poop. Though he couldn't smell it, flies had started picking up on the odors, becoming something of a nuisance. Sometimes, one of the predators would catch a fly that had landed, or a bobcat would bat one out of the air.

On the next Tuesday morning, the old man readied his trunk with a new batch of figurines and prepared to leave. Just like the previous week, his animals sat and watched him get ready. Once again, he felt apprehensive about leaving them behind. He considered bringing along one of the bears but decided against it. No one would believe his story about creating live animals, and there would be a thousand questions about how he did it.

With a shiver, he crossed the narrow yard to the waiting truck and climbed in.

Upon reaching Jimmie's store, he found the back door locked. He knocked a few times, but no one answered. Puzzled, he walked around to the front door. Just as he reached it, a young man came out, locking the door behind him. It was Jess, Jimmie's part-time employee.

"Oh, hi," Jess said, turning to face the old man.

Glowering under the brim of his hat, the old man asked, "What's going on? What's wrong with Jimmie?"

Jess stammered, "J-Jimmie's sick. He's been out since last Friday. He asked me to check on the live bait and make sure everything's okay."

"Did he say anything about buying more of my animals?"

"Nah, not a word. He'll probably be back by Thursday or Friday. He said he thought he was on the mend."

The old man's face clouded over like a storm. "Gah!" He turned and walked back to his truck.

Why did Jimmie have to rely on kids like Jess? All they wanted to do was fish and hunt after school. He slammed the tailgate with his palm and climbed into the truck. He pulled out his wallet to check how much cash he had—twenty-five dollars. Enough for lunch but not for more animal food. He hated the thought of coming back on Friday, but his animals would need to be fed. Putting his truck into gear, he left the parking lot and headed toward Johnny's Log Bar. It was a bit early, but that was okay—he didn't usually eat much before coming to town.

He parked in front of Johnny's and went inside. The air conditioning felt good, easing some of his tension. He took his seat by the window.

A waitress in a white dress uniform came over with a glass of water for him. "Do you need a menu? And what would you like to drink?" She was young and pretty with black hair, though her voice was scratchy. With a sigh, he said, "I'll have my usual."

The waitress paused. "And that would be . . . ?"

Sharply, the old man barked, "Is Shayna here? She always knows what I want!"

"Uh, no. She doesn't work here anymore. She died." "Huh? Oh . . . I'm . . . I'm sorry. How . . . ?"

"Heart attack last Wednesday. Do you know what you want?" she pressed.

"Funeral?"

"Yesterday." There was a brief pause. "Do you need more time?"

Shaken, he managed to say, "A Western omelet, wheat toast, a dish of applesauce, a hamburger, and a Guinness."

With an odd look on her face, the waitress moved to the kitchen to place the order. The old man just sat there, lost in thought. Shayna had been a part of his routine for years. Her death disrupted that routine with the same gut-wrenching angst as any loss of something familiar. She was gone. What was he going to do now?

He waited for his meal to come, but his mind raced with thoughts of his loss, his new family of animals, and the food they needed. He wondered how much longer it would take. It felt like forever. With his eyes closed, he sat rigidly, like a volcano ready to explode, when the scratchy voice announced, "Here you are."

The waitress set the plates down and carefully placed the Guinness in front of him. "Anything else?"

He waved her away without a word. She left, wondering what kind of tip she'd get.

Slowly, he took a sip of the Guinness. His Tuesday meal was the only time he splurged, buying and drinking a Guinness. Being served by Shayna had been part of the ritual, and now she was gone. The loss disturbed him on so many levels. He lifted the omelet to see underneath it, hoping—no, *expecting*—to find the burnt match. But it wasn't there.

The absence of the match hit him harder than he had anticipated. It had started as a simple mistake, a burnt match hidden under his sandwich at the 7th Street Grill. When he'd told Shayna about it, she had turned it into a joke—a well-meaning joke that became a ritual every time he ordered the omelet. It had become an important part of their interaction, a small but meaningful tradition. And now, it was gone, just like she was.

The burnt match was missing. The world felt like it was crumbling around him despite his miraculous discovery of clay and live animals. So attached had he become to his Tuesday ritual with Shayna that it felt like something vital had been taken away. He picked at his meal, but it tasted bland and unappealing. He was nearly finished with his Guinness when an elderly woman approached him.

He had noticed her when he entered Johnnie's—tall and slender, with long brown-and-gray hair, wearing nice tailored clothes, and a slight smile on her face. Now, she was advancing toward him, and he felt a bit apprehensive. Waitresses were one thing, but a complete stranger? That was another.

"Hi, excuse me," she said. "I understand you're the one who's been creating the wildlife figurines I've seen in the stores here. Do you mind if I sit down with you?" He nodded slightly but kept his eye on her as she slid effortlessly into the booth across from him.

"I wanted to compliment you on how beautifully you've made the animals. They look so real, you might think they could walk or fly away. My name is Bonnie," she added softly.

He nodded again, mustering a faint, "Thank you."

"How do you do it?" Bonnie continued, her smile never faltering. "You've captured every detail of the bear, the beaver—all of them."

Feeling less threatened, the old man relaxed a bit. "I've always been a good observer. I see things that others miss or ignore." He paused for a moment, then, feeling more at ease, added, "I've been making these animals for many years now. Plenty of practice. It's just who I am."

Bonnie continued smiling, nodding her head as the conversation carried on. They spoke briefly about his artistry, and she complimented his carvings, mentioning how she'd seen other works that didn't come close to his quality.

There was something about Bonnie that unsettled him. She was both familiar and distant as if parts of her were buried under layers of time. He responded to her mostly with one-word answers, but he couldn't shake the odd feeling she stirred in him. Her pleasant voice, smooth yet strangely detached, seemed at odds with the hand movements he kept noticing. It was her name too—something about it triggered an uncomfortable recognition deep inside him.

"YOU!" he said, his voice heavy with disbelief. His spine shot straight, and he sat upright in the booth. "You!" he repeated more forcefully.

Bonnie leaned back, her faint smile shifting into something harder, almost knowing. "I wondered how long it would take for you to remember," she replied, the smoothness of her voice slipping into something colder.

"How . . . how . . . ?" he stammered, his hands trembling. "Why?"

His face twisted with amazement and doubt as confusion rippled through him.

"I've been here for three days, wandering through old places . . . places we came to when we were still in love." Bonnie sighed, her voice tinged with something else—longing? Disappointment? "I wanted to see what you'd become, see if you'd made anything of yourself. I knew you were still in Baldwin, and I knew you'd stay stuck in the same small, predictable life."

"Why?" he asked again, trying to grasp the meaning behind her words. "Curiosity," Bonnie said flatly, her eyes hardening. "I skimmed through

the *Baldwin Gazette*, looking for signs of you, hoping for something. But nothing. Absolutely nothing." She paused, letting the silence hang between them. "Do you want to know what I've been doing since I left?"

The old man leaned back against his seat, faintly shaking his head no, almost as if to escape. "No," he whispered.

But she continued anyway. "When I left you . . . when I left Baldwin, I was lost. Drowning in regret. I hated everything about what we had, including falling in love with *you*."

She exhaled sharply. "So I left. Packed my bags and ran to California, away from everything that reminded me of you. When I got there, I did just that. I parked my car and ran down to the beach and plunged into the Pacific Ocean, clothes and all. It was glorious, freeing. When I dried off, I found a crappy apartment and got a job at a boutique. Now, I own the business and make my own line of clothes. I employ thirty people."

She placed a business card on the table, her fingers brushing the edge. He glanced at it but didn't pick it up. "And I came back here to see what you'd done. Your little animals. They're . . . marvelous," she said, the word tainted with a bitter edge.

The old man swallowed the last of his Guinness, his stomach uneasy. "I've got to go," he muttered, sliding out of the booth. The young waitress called after him. "Wait, I've got your bill!"

He didn't turn back. He found his truck and sped away, heading back to his place. At his place, he didn't even bother putting the truck in the garage. He entered through the back door, greeted by the usual noise of his animals. Their calls—grunts, barks, squawks—filled the air. Hungry, restless. He opened cans of chicken for the dogs, then scattered bread crumbs for the ducks and geese. They were satisfied for now, but the deer, elk, and moose were still waiting.

He noticed his mistake and hurried outside to gather grass and leaves. He returned, spreading the food. The animals calmed fed.

But then, the door to the front of the store creaked open. Someone had entered quietly, moving around the floor, the lid of the pop cooler rising and falling.

"Who's there?" he called, his voice tight with unease. No reply.

His animals were shifting restlessly, moving nervously as though sensing his apprehension. The ducks and geese began to wander aimlessly, their eyes darting to the corner where he stood.

Suddenly, the curtain that separated the store from the studio was pulled back. Bonnie stood there, surveying the room with a cold look in her eyes.

He turned sharply. "What are you doing here? What do you want?"

Her gaze fixed on him, and the tension in the air thickened. "I don't want anything. I just wanted to see my store. My once-upon-a-time home," she said, her voice flat and bitter. "But now, I see it's a disgrace."

"What do you mean 'your store'? You left. You haven't lived here for decades."

Bonnie stepped closer, her face hard. "True. But tell me, how do you keep the lights on? How do you pay for the heating oil? Who covers the taxes? Who keeps this dump afloat? I do. It's mine."

The old man's face contorted in disbelief.

"We bought this together! Our names are on the deed."

"You left. You left me!"

"Did I?" Bonnie laughed bitterly. "I didn't leave you. I watched you bury your dreams—your potential. You drowned them in your own ego, never caring for anything or anyone but yourself." She moved closer, her eyes digging into his soul. "I ran this place while you sat on your art. I kept you alive with my money, my effort, my sweat. And what did I get in return? Nothing."

Her voice broke like glass, but it only pushed him further.

"You never had any talent. You clung to mine, riding on my coattails, pretending to be an artist." His voice rose with growing anger. "You were just a shopkeeper. Nothing more."

Bonnie's face twisted with fury. She grabbed a lump of clay and threw it at him.

He stumbled backward, enraged. She took another chunk of clay and flung it at him again. This time, it hit him square in the chest, and he fell.

Unnoticed by either of them, the live animals around the room had begun to growl, roar, and paw the ground, growing more agitated. As the old man tried to stand again, swearing, the animals advanced on Bonnie. The geese and ducks took flight and began flying about her head. It took a moment for her to focus on them, but then she started swatting at them. The dozen or so birds dove at her, flapping into her eyes and nipping at her with their beaks. The two eagles flew down and raked her exposed skin with their talons. She held up one arm in front of her face and caught one of the ducks with a swipe of her other hand, knocking it to the floor hard. The duck didn't move and, within seconds, crumbled into a pile of dust.

The old man had been watching the whole scene, seething with anger yet amazed that the birds had attacked Bonnie. But when he saw the duck crumble apart, a new wave of anger rose. Snarling, he got to his feet. He looked at her again, now raising and slapping at her feet and ankles. The other animals had attacked, also. The wolves and bears were nipping hard on her ankles while the deer, elk, and moose jammed against her feet and any opening on her ankles. Wearing slip-ons, Bonnie's feet, exposed to the ravages of the animals, were bleeding. Losing her balance while slapping her feet and trying to keep the birds out of her face, she toppled over one of the chairs in the crowded studio, falling to the floor. More exposed now to the predators, they began attacking her all over, but especially her neck, while the birds continued to mainly go for her head. Shrieking now, she continued struggling but to no avail. Some of the wolves had bit so hard on her fingers and hands that she lifted them off the floor. Pools of blood were appearing around her feet, ankles, and neck; her face was streaked with gashes and blood. The animals continued attacking until she lay still.

The old man had stood watching the spectacle in awe. He was still angry but also surprised and even scared of what he just saw play out. Now that Bonnie wasn't struggling anymore, the animals backed off, though they were still agitated, growling and snapping at each other. A couple of piles of crumbled clay signaled to him that Bonnie managed to kill some of the animals, though he wasn't sure which ones. He was beginning to feel loss, but whether it was for Bonnie or the deceased animals, he didn't know.

Coming out of his daze, he went to Bonnie, knelt beside her, searching for a pulse. He couldn't find one. He sat back on the floor while his remaining animals milled about, looking at both Bonnie's body and at him. They no longer seemed agitated, though they were closely watching him. His anger slowly receded. He thought about Bonnie, trying to come to grips with their early life, but more importantly, why she had come back. Reviewing their conversation at the bar, he pieced together that even though she had left him, she thought he might achieve something. She had invested a lot of money over time in keeping him going and wanted to see what she had gotten in return. It probably gnawed at her that she was still somewhat concerned about his well-being despite despising him. But she didn't need to ridicule him for his artistic work. Granted, he hadn't produced a masterpiece of painting or sculpture, yet he had been busy selling a few things over the years. And had stumbled onto his animal figurines.

Over time, the gross of money they produced was probably a lot. But he didn't care about that. He had his work, his hermit lifestyle, he had required little of the outside world. But now Bonnie was gone. The loss he felt before now grew, and he knew he had now truly lost her. He knew they had been in love for a while, that coming to Baldwin had been part of a dream, solitude where creative minds could come up with whatever they wanted. Maybe she did have talent, but it wasn't overly impressive, not compared to him. He felt that the world would beat a path to their place because of him, not her. And so the separation began.

His animals had now calmed down and sat or lay in places all over the studio, patiently waiting for him. Looking about, he tried to count the animals but stopped once he reached 100. For a brief time, he had been amazingly prolific. He had gotten the feeling that they were connected to him mentally. He couldn't understand how it happened or why the newly found clay warmed his hands, his whole body, while he worked with it. But it had been wonderful creating these creatures. He was saddened that he had lost at least three animals today.

He turned his attention back to Bonnie. He leaned over and stroked her hair. Blood had crusted here and there. Her face was unrecognizable. Deep in his heart, he knew he was alone now, more alone than ever before. Over the years, he had forgotten about her, but somewhere deep inside, he knew she was out there, somewhere. Now, she would no longer be anywhere. And then a new realization hit him: if she had been paying all the bills over the years, how would he survive here? He had no idea how to proceed. How did she pay the bills, and who to? He had become totally dependent on her without knowing it. This drove a cold dagger into his heart. His pulse quickened. How was he going to survive? He'd no longer be able to create anything or any more of his animals. Panicking, he shook her shoulder as if to wake her up, to no avail.

Breathing hard, he stood up and paced around the studio. The animals became agitated once again. He stomped out into the store and, for the first time in many years, looked at the empty shelves and the few snack things on the counter. The soda pop cooler hummed in one corner, but without electricity, that would stop. Without electricity, he wouldn't be able to create more live animals. What was he thinking? The loneliness he felt earlier was beginning to overwhelm him. Reality was hammering his mind. He stormed back into the studio. All the animals were alert and at attention. He turned around, facing all of them.

"You—YOU did this to me," he shouted at the animals, his voice ragged with fury. "And I let you do it!"

He smashed a chair with his foot and pulled off one of the chair's legs. Raising it up, he started swinging it like a baseball bat. He caught the first two animals by surprise, two of the geese sitting on a shelf. They were crushed and soon became dust. The other animals began to creep toward him while the birds flew up above him to begin diving at him. This made the old man even more angry, and as a result, all the animals viciously attacked him. He continued swinging the leg, trying to hit more of the birds, but his aim was off. The birds attacked him as they had with Bonnie, swooping down into his face, smacking his eyes with their wings, and pecking him as they flew by. The eagles raked his face.

The other animals attacked his bare ankles. Two of the bears climbed up to the shelves on the wall, and when he fell back against the shelf, the bears jumped onto his shoulders and started biting his shoulders and neck. He continued swinging the leg but was hitting nothing. He teetered, then fell. Thrashing and yelling more than ever, he tried to defend himself, but it was short-lived. He suddenly knew that it was over. He was finished. The world would never honor him. He dropped his arms; the chair leg fell out of his hand, and he lay there while the animals he had created finished the job. The bears, wolves, foxes, moose, deer, elk, and all the rest soon quieted down, no longer fueled by the old man's anger. One by one, they laid down where they were, and appearing to sleep, they all cracked and crumbled into piles of clay dust.

A couple of days later, one of the locals noticed that the same car had been sitting in front of the store now for three days, which was highly unusual. One of the hunters stopped and cautiously walked up to the door. It was unlocked, and he stepped in. There was a rank odor, but he saw that the storefront was empty. Moving back to the curtain and pulling it open, the smell became much stronger. He saw the two bodies.

The police arrived and began the investigation into what had happened. Photographs were taken, but there was no indication of shots being fired. The county coroner was called in. What was remarkable was the damage done to the face, neck, hands, arms, feet, and ankles. Bemused, the coroner commented that he had never seen anything like this. It was like the victims were nibbled to death. Maybe rats chewed the bodies? Obviously, autopsies would be performed. What also was puzzling were the piles of dirt or dust scattered about the room, a couple hundred was the guess. Photographs were taken.

As the coroner was about to leave, one of the policemen asked, "Hey, doc, do you want a pop?" The coroner nodded, and the officer pulled two bottles out of the humming soda pop cooler.

The next day, the headline in the *Baldwin Gazette* read, "Local artist, estranged wife found dead."

Two days later, a fierce rainstorm dumped several inches overnight, leading to the flooding of local streams. The stream behind the artist's store had been particularly flooded. Debris and sediment carried from upstream added to the beaver dam burying the one end of the pond where the clay was now under feet of sediment.

After the probate process, the store and studio were auctioned off, and the building was torn down. A souvenir shop was built, with one wall sporting the animal figurines that the old man had made and was credited with. The soda pop cooler had been saved because it was considered an antique and ran quietly in the corner of the new shop.

Lucille's Case

It was around 10:00 am when Lucille's phone rang. Lucille worked as a social worker at the city's Children Services Office, and as usual, she was swamped with routine paperwork. She wasn't in a hurry to answer the phone. Eventually, the ringing became more annoying than the paperwork, so in her best, though somewhat grumpy manner, she grabbed the handset from the cradle. As she reached for the phone, she quickly thought that the donut next to her coffee would be the next thing snatched up. She wasn't overweight, just a little pudgy.

"Good morning, Lucille here," she muttered, half growling, half purring.

It was Maddie, the office receptionist, telling Lucille that she had a woman on hold who desperately needed to speak with a caseworker. Lucille mentally sighed. Everyone seemed desperate these days. What about herself? Wasn't she desperate too?

Nevertheless, she agreed to take the call, and the receptionist connected her with the woman who identified herself as Marcie, waiting patiently as Lucille gathered up a note pad and pencil.

"Okay, Marcie, how can I help you?" Lucille was all business now and would attempt to read all the undercurrents in the caller's voice to try to assess her stress level, just how desperate she was, and what was causing the stress.

"It's my son," Marcie said quietly. "I have reached a point where I need help to . . . to . . . cope with him." Marcie's voice was calm, somewhat matter of fact, even polite, but Lucille had the impression that Marcie's psyche was stretched like cellophane over a salad bowl sitting in a refrigerator. In a distant part of her brain, Lucille wondered why she thought of a salad bowl. It was way too early for lunch.

"Your son?" Lucille replied. "What is your son doing or not doing, Marcie, that made you call me?"

"I—well, he . . . he's just being himself. Sort of. I mean, it's hard to explain over the phone . . ." Marcie's voice trailed off.

Frowning, Lucille pressed on. "What do you mean 'he's being himself'?

Is he doing drugs? Being abusive? But first things first, Marcie—how old is your son?"

"He's eleven. And no, he doesn't do drugs. No, no, that's not the problem at all. And he isn't abusive. Todd is a wonderful little boy, full of life, and very loving."

And *this* is the problem, Lucille thought.

"Marcie, I guess I don't understand what the problem is. Can you help me out? Is he a special needs child?"

"Well, yes and no. If you mean, is he handicapped? No, no, he isn't." Marcie paused, then continued in a quiet, intense voice. "He is special. He's very special."

The headache that had been growing in Lucille's forehead now threatened to take over her whole head. Okay, there we have it, she thought. Marcie is desperate because her eleven-year-old son is *special*. Good Lord.

"Marcie, dear. I've been having a rough morning, and this conversation isn't helping. Please tell me what you're so desperate about, or I'm going to have to hang up the phone and beat myself with my cane. I'm sure you don't want that, so please—just spit it out."

"Well . . . okay . . . uh . . . My son, Todd, he can . . . well, he can do magic." Marcie's polite voice was now beginning to shake. Lucille noticed the change. Whatever she meant by *magic*, the cellophane was about to snap.

In a more soothing tone, Lucille replied, "Now, Marcie, everything will be all right. Just let me ask you a couple more questions. What do you mean by magic? Todd can do card tricks? Or pull coins out of people's ears?"

"No, no, nothing like that." Marcie's voice quickly became shrill. "Have you ever had a full-grown elephant in your living room? Have you ever had a giant bunny eating your house plants? Have you ever had a jungle growing in your bathroom? Have you ever had to explain to your neighbors and the police why your car was resting on top of theirs? How many more questions would you like to ask me?" Marcie was practically shrieking now.

Lucille stared at the phone handset in confusion. The only response she could manage was, "Hunh?"

It was clear Marcie was struggling to keep calm, her breath coming in heavy gulps.

"Marcie, honey, I . . . I don't know what to say to your questions, but . . . but I think it might be best if I came to your home to see for myself." Lucille considered that perhaps Todd had something to fear from his mother.

"Yes, yes, please, can you come today?"

Lucille quickly jotted down Marcie's address and phone number. She hadn't worked much in that part of town before. After hanging up, she glanced around the office, wondering who could give her a rundown of the area. She spotted a large map of the city on the back wall. She took a bite of her donut, grabbed her cane, and made her way over to it. The cane hadn't been a joke. Lucille found it useful to help her hip pain and garner sympathy.

St. John sat at his desk near the map, watching Lucille as she made her way toward him. He respected Lucille for being a tireless worker, but he never crossed her. Her tongue had earned a wide reputation for its sting. As she passed his desk, the two exchanged glances from the corner of their eyes, like two cats, each anticipating an attack from the other.

Lucille studied the map for a moment. "St. John, do you know anything about the Arrington neighborhood? What kind of people do we have growing over there? And remind me again, why the hell do we call you St. John?"

John hoped to blend in with his desk, trying to become invisible like one of those octopuses on the nature channel. But it didn't work. "I don't know. I mean, my nickname . . . Someone called me that one day, and someone else overheard it, and it stuck."

"Too bad," she grumbled, turning back to the map. "I don't suppose you know anything about the 'hood'?" Lucille spoke with her back to John.

John moved beside her to take a look at the map. "Yeah, I've been through there a few times. It's nice enough—a mix of lower to upper-middle class, sort of a 1950s-style neighborhood. Quiet. Not many calls from there . . ."

"Paradise on earth, hmm?" Lucille growled.

"Well, I guess . . . maybe . . . ," John hesitated.

"Okay, St. Johnny. I'm off. If anyone asks where I am, tell them I have a ticket for a magic show." Lucille limped back to her desk, threw a few papers into her bag, grabbed her cane, and was out the door.

The drive to the Arrington neighborhood was uneventful. Lucille yelled at only two other motorists—a good day, as far as she was concerned. Hastings Avenue was a quiet street through the more distant part of Arrington. She found the address Marcie had given her, but the house was barely visible because of the high wooden fence surrounding the yard.

"Looks ominous," Lucille thought as she parked.

She got out of her car and walked to the fence gate. She glanced up and down the street but didn't see anyone else. "Johnny boy was right. This is a quiet place." The other homes were well-landscaped, and the yards were relatively large. "My grandson could get a lot of mowing jobs here," she thought.

The gate was locked. Lucille thumped on the fence with her cane, but eventually, she had to resort to calling the number Marcie had given her.

"Hello?"

"Marcie? Lucille here. I can't seem to find the right key to open your gate. Would you be a dear and come open it for me so I can come in?" Lucille added, "You do still want to talk, don't you?"

Marcie apologized and promised she'd be right there. Three or four minutes later, Lucille heard someone coming out the front door and light footsteps approaching the gate. Three intricate deadbolts slid back, and the gate opened.

"Hi, I'm Lucille from Family Services," Lucille said in a light, professional tone. "You must be Marcie."

Marcie was a woman in her forties, about 5'4", slender, even athletic, with medium-length mousey brown hair. She wore jeans and a long-sleeved, buttoned-down shirt, untucked. Her pink Nike shoes enhanced her athletic appearance. Otherwise, Marcie was unremarkable. Lucille noted that she probably wouldn't be able to describe her to anyone later, as Marcie was otherwise very plain. She was polite in inviting Lucille into the yard and apologized for taking so long to open the gate. Apparently, it was a long walk from the kitchen.

Lucille surveyed the yard and house. How big was this place? It didn't look that big. Maybe she hadn't heard Marcie correctly.

Lucille followed Marcie up a couple of steps to the front door. As Marcie began to open it, she hesitated and glanced nervously at Lucille. "Uh, don't be surprised at what you see," she said apologetically.

Marcie pushed the door open and stood back for Lucille to enter. The brightness outside made Lucille's eyes take a moment to adjust. When they did, Lucille was awe-struck. The foyer opened into a cavernous hall, like something you'd expect to see in a castle. Candles and torches were strategically placed along the walls. Tables and chairs were scattered throughout the room. Shields, spears, and swords hung on the walls. At the far end of the hall, a large fireplace cast a crimson light, creating eerie shadows throughout the space. Dumbfounded, Lucille gaped at the size of the room—hall, whatever you wanted to call it.

"Uh, just a minute, please, Marcie." Lucille stepped back out onto the narrow front porch. She first looked down one side of the house, then walked to the other end of the porch and looked down that side. The headache that had been subdued by a cup of coffee on the drive over to Marcie's house had gained new strength and was advancing on her whole head again.

Turning back to the front door, she stepped inside once more. She turned to Marcie. "How'd you do this? What is this place?"

"This is my foyer/receiving room," Marcie said. "Todd decided we needed more space, and so—poof! There it was."

"Todd, the eleven-year-old, did this?" Lucille asked, stunned.

Marcie closed her eyes tightly, pursed her lips, and nodded silently.

"But . . . how?" Lucille's senses reeled. She couldn't believe what she saw.

Jingy by jinggies, what had she gotten herself into?

Marcie took Lucille's right hand and led her to a nearby table. A torch blazed cheerfully above the table. "Please, sit down. I'll get us some drinks. Do you like lemonade?"

Lucille mumbled something, but looking around the room, she seemed lost. Marcie guided her into a comfortable, well-padded chair next to the dark wood table and excused herself. Lucille glanced around the hall. Aside from the ornaments hanging on the walls, there was nothing else—no pictures, no TV, and no photographs except for one on an end table: a man, a woman, and a baby in arms. Lucille suspected it was this family.

A few minutes later, Marcie returned with two glasses of lemonade. During her absence, Lucille had tried to pull herself together. *Marcie was desperate . . . she had called the office asking for help . . .* Lucille reminded herself she was here to help.

"So, uh, Marcie . . . how"—Lucille shook her head—"when did Todd start . . ."

Marcie interjected, "When did Todd begin to use magic?" She sighed. "When he was about one and a half years old, my husband and I bought Todd a white stuffed kitty with long fur. Todd loved that kitty and took it to bed with him for every nap and at bedtime. When he was about two, I went into the nursery to get him up and dressed, and when I pulled his blanket back, his kitty turned its head to look at me . . . and it was purring. Todd loved his kitty and took it everywhere with him. Then things began to appear for his kitty to play with—balls, pieces of yarn, live mice."

Lucille raised an eyebrow, doubtful. Marcie quickly added, "No, we didn't buy any of those things for his kitty—they just appeared. We never knew what we'd find in his bed each morning.

"Todd had Kitty Kat—that's what he called it—for a couple of years, until he became interested in other animals. He started watching TV and got some of his ideas from there. One day, an alligator appeared in the wading pool in the backyard. Todd was thrilled—he'd been watching a program about alligators and made one—about five feet long. Unfortunately, the alligator snatched and ate his kitty. Todd was so angry that he turned the alligator into a ball and kicked it all over the yard for the next week. The next time Todd saw an alligator on TV, the alligator unexpectedly died . . . on TV.

"That was when we decided maybe Todd shouldn't watch TV—or at least only approved programs. But that turned out to still be a disaster. Do you know how funny a five-year-old thinks it is to have buckets, gallons, and DRUMS of green slime fall out of the ceiling onto you? Do you?!"

Marcie was only half Lucille's size, but Lucille was becoming scared of her. At least now, she understood why there was no TV. The bugged-out eyes and red cheeks receded as Marcie regained her calm.

"Lucille, I can't take it anymore. I don't know what to do. I've homeschooled Todd, tried to protect him from himself—and tried to protect the neighbors."

Lucille's mouth fell open as she listened, more and more astounded by what Marcie had shared. Right now, beating herself with her cane seemed like a reasonable response to what she was hearing. But Lucille got a grip on her wits.

"You keep saying 'we.' So what about your husband? Where is he in all of this?"

"Uh, well, Rob passed away three years ago."

"I'm sorry to hear that, Marcie," Lucille said, genuinely. "What happened? Illness? Car accident?"

"It was a work accident. Have you heard of the Knowlton Toy Factory? No? Well, they made unusual toys—special order sorts of things, sometimes more than just kid toys. Rob was an engineer, and the project he was working on was a life-size model of a catapult. There was a problem—it wasn't firing properly. Rob was checking it out when one of the other workers accidentally hit the trigger thingy, and the bucket caught him and flung him into the air . . . through the second-floor windows. There was a cement mixer driving past the factory, and apparently, Rob . . ." Marcie's voice cracked as she started tearing up. "Well, he landed in the mixing tank. They never found his body. The police think Rob is in the foundation of a new high-rise apartment building a few blocks from the toy factory." Marcie's voice dropped to a whisper, choking with emotion.

Lucille's expression changed from concern to amazement.

The image of a man being flung through a window from a *toy* catapult, landing in a moving cement mixer, and then being poured into a foundation was terrible. A horrible coincidence, yet excruciatingly funny. Lucille grimaced and squirmed in her chair, reminding herself that it was a tragic accident—Marcie lost her husband, and a child grew up without his father—but it was also one of the funniest things Lucille had ever heard. Tears ran down both of their cheeks, for entirely different reasons.

Lucille took a deep breath, collected her professional composure, dabbed at her tears, and trying hard to keep a straight face, reached out to take Marcie's hand. A few sobs later, Marcie had pulled herself together for the second time.

"I'm sorry for my breakdown," Marcie said, dabbing her tears with a tissue. "Thank you for your patience."

Lucille comforted her as best as she could, then, after a brief pause, said,

"Maybe I should meet Todd?" Actually, Lucille dreaded the idea, but she was a professional—and this is what a professional does.

"Oh, of course. I think he's in his room. Just a minute." Marcie went to a part of the wall where a brightly colored phone hung. She didn't dial a number—she simply picked up the receiver and asked Todd to join them in the front hall. Marcie smiled faintly as she hung up the receiver.

"Todd's idea."

"I see. Todd seems to be a creative eleven-year-old."

Marcie cleared her throat. "Yes, very creative." She wasn't smiling.

When Todd came into the hall, he was carrying something bright. It resolved into a bouquet of flowers for his mother. Lucille noticed that Todd was an unremarkable kid—maybe a little tall, but otherwise looked and acted like a normal sandy-haired eleven-year-old boy.

"My, what a wonderful bunch of flowers, Todd," said Marcie. "Where did you get them?"

"My garden."

Marcie looked puzzled.

"In my bathroom. I don't want to take baths anymore, so I started a garden where the bathtub was," Todd said matter-of-factly.

"But, Todd, honey . . . you must take baths. How are you going to get clean? You know, the warm water feels so good, and when you add the soap, well, you can imagine all sorts of things in the tub with the bubbly suds." Marcie's reasoning was sweet, but Lucille could see the smile was artificial, and Marcie's jaw muscles were clenched.

"Well, I can just wish away the dirt. I don't like the way water feels sometimes. But maybe I'll take a bath sometime, just not today. Would you like to see my garden?" Todd then noticed Lucille.

"Who are you?"

Lucille straightened up and said pleasantly, "My name is Lucille. How are you today?"

Todd smiled briefly. "I ask the questions here. It's my job to protect me and my mother. Why are you here?" Todd's face took on a serious expression. Lucille felt a trickle of nervousness run down her spine.

"I just stopped by to see your mother and talk about things."

Unfortunately, Todd caught the quick sideways glance Lucille gave Marcie.

"Who are you, Lucille? My mother never talks about you." He turned to Marcie. "Who is this lady, Mother?"

"Uh, well, I asked Lucille here to . . . talk about things, that maybe you and I might be able to do." She sounded hopeful.

"Like what?"

"I don't know yet, honey. We've just begun to talk. Why don't you take care of the flowers and go play with your train set while we talk? But first, take care of the flowers, please?"

Obediently, Todd held out his hand, and a flower vase appeared. He placed the flowers in it.

"Remember the water."

Todd made a face, as if saying, *Oh yeah, I forgot,* and water filled the vase. He waved his hand, and a small wooden table appeared next to Marcie. Todd gently placed the flowers and vase on the table.

"That's fine, honey. Thank you. Go play." Marcie smiled, and without another word, Todd skipped away, shouting, "Choo choo!"

Marcie turned back to Lucille, who was sitting across from her, mouth agape and wide-eyed. "Did Todd just do what I saw him do?"

"What do you mean?" Marcie hissed. She reached out, grabbing Lucille's hand, her grip tightening as she spoke. "He's a sweet, loving little boy who is driving me insane! How does he do that? I don't know! Why does he do the things he does? I don't know!" Marcie was losing control again.

Lucille sat there, dumbfounded. Her eyes were wide, and Marcie's grip was starting to hurt her hand. Her headache had turned into a loud, rhythmic beating that she finally realized was her pulse.

"Uh, I don't know what to say . . ." Lucille fumbled for words, a rarity for her. "This is way above my pay grade. I can deal with child abuse, broken homes, and so on. But . . . but this," she stammered, "I have no idea where to go from here. Maybe the best bet would be for a child psychologist to step in. I have some sources back in my office"—she wrinkled her brow—"on my rolodex? Let me see what I can do." She wasn't sure she could convince anyone that an eleven-year-old could make flower vases, water, and wooden tables appear out of nowhere—all within a medieval hall larger than the house's exterior.

In a bit of a rush, Lucille excused herself, packing up her briefcase and purse. Marcie looked forlorn. "When will you get back to me?"

"As soon as I can, Marcie. It'll take time for phone calls. I'll let you know."

"Please, Lucille, don't tell anyone about Todd's abilities. Especially not the police. Todd doesn't like them, and, well, they don't like coming here. Strange things happen, like their guns turning into chocolate bars." Marcie was wringing her hands, her expression pleading.

"Yeah, right!" Lucille thought. She leaned over and gave Marcie a brief hug.

Marcie followed Lucille to the door, and once more, Lucille looked both ways outside the house, mumbling something like, "Shit if I know how he does it."

Marcie quickly closed the gate behind Lucille and slid the three dead bolts into place. Lucille let out a long breath, realizing just how tense she'd been. Getting into her car, her mind raced. Todd seemed like a nice kid, but protective of his mother. For someone who could do magic like he did, what did that mean? If someone said something nasty to his mother, would that person end up in a tree? Or turned into a rug? The possibilities seemed endless, and the more she thought about it, the more she hyperventilated.

Wait, what am I doing, getting all hyped up? she thought. She never did that. She always had control of the situation. Except now, she knew of a kid who could produce an alligator out of thin air and turn it into a ball. She'd never had to deal with that before. Engrossed in her thoughts while driving back to her office, Lucille ran a red light. One of the city's finest quickly brought her back to the present.

"Sorry, Officer"—she shrugged—"bad day."

"Don't we all?" the officer replied, handing her the ticket.

As the officer walked back to his car, the thought of a chocolate gun made Lucille feel a little better.

When Lucille returned to her office, she was in a grumbly mood again. Ticket be damned! She walked with her cane down the hallway, and a passerby gave her a wide berth. She snarled as her phone rang just as she sat down. The caller quickly apologized for asking such a trivial question. Lucille grunted and then noticed she had three missed calls. The first two she tossed into the trash, but the third one she stared at for a minute, sighed, and dialed the number. It was one of her other cases that would take up the rest of her day.

After work, she headed home to her modest little house, with its flower beds and a couple of overhanging trees. She needed to unwind and rarely thought about work while at home. As she prepared her supper, she had Alexa play smooth jazz. The music had her swaying and swishing around within minutes. Later, a friend stopped by, and by 10:30, Lucille was ready for bed. But before turning in, she tuned in to the local news. Initially, all she could say about the various stories was, "Stupid politicians."

But when she saw the news alert about an explosion in the Arrington part of town, she looked closer. A neighbor's phone video showed a glowing cloud of smoke rising high above a tall wooden fence. It was unknown what had caused the explosion, and by the time the first responders arrived, everything appeared fine. No damage could be seen, and everything was tranquil. But everyone in the neighborhood had heard the explosion. On camera, a middle-aged woman named Marcie was asked about it. Yes, she had heard it but didn't know what caused it, and no, they didn't have any damage. Lucille looked closely—Marcie was standing there, speaking with reporters while tightly gripping Todd's shoulders, who stood in front of her. Todd's face was blurred out, but Lucille could see that neither of them looked comfortable. The reporter went on to say that other unusual events had occurred in Arrington over the past few years, with no known causes.

Going to bed, Lucille was restless, having weird dreams of magicians. She snapped awake when one of the magicians opened a box on a table, revealing her smiling head inside.

By the time Lucille reached her office the next morning, there was already a stack of missed calls. One she immediately tossed into the trash, another she could deal with quickly, and two from Marcie. Not a surprise. Grabbing another cup of coffee and a donut from the box on her desk, she quickly dealt with one of the calls.

Almost dreading the next call, Lucille bit off a chunk of apple fritter for fortification and dialed Marcie's number.

Marcie answered and immediately snapped, "Did you see the news last night?"

"Uh, yes I did, Marcie," Lucille responded slowly and calmly. "What happened?"

Marcie explained that someone had thrown a firecracker over their fence. Todd had found it and wondered what it was. She started to tell him what it did but then realized that was a mistake. She took it away and disposed of it. But Todd remained outside and tried to make his own firecracker, not realizing how strong it would be. He managed to set it off, blasting a shallow hole in the backyard. Fortunately, he had tossed it before it blew, but he was knocked off his feet anyway. At least he wasn't hurt, just scared. Marcie convinced him that he needed to repair the yard and any other damage immediately, or all hell was coming his way. As a mother, Marcie still had some influence on Todd's behavior. By the time first responders arrived, Todd had patched everything up.

Thank goodness, thought Lucille. She was relieved that Marcie still had control over Todd—it was fantastic. She didn't want to think about how things would work out when that ended.

"Lucille, did you find a child psychologist?" Marcie demanded.

With a sigh, Lucille replied that she hadn't had the time, but today that would be her priority. After hanging up, Lucille delved into her rolodex looking for a psychologist—any psychologist, let alone one who specialized in children. She knew she was a relic, relying on something as ancient as a rolodex, but it worked for her, and she didn't have to spend her *precious* time learning computer stuff.

She came across three names. Two she knew and had worked with before. Unfortunately, both were unavailable. The first was buried under work and wouldn't be able to meet with Marcie and Todd until sometime the following week. The other, Frank, would like to help her out, but he was going on vacation for two weeks and was buried in trying to catch up on his workload before leaving. Frank mentioned that there was a new guy, Eric Swan, who might be a good fit. Glancing at the third rolodex card, she realized she had recently added him to her deck.

With another sigh, Lucille dialed Eric's number. While waiting for the phone to ring, she wondered how many times a day she sighed. Whatever the number, it probably wouldn't be the last one regarding Todd and Marcie. "Hello, Eric Swan here." Eric's voice sounded nasal and pinched.

"Hi, Eric, my name is Lucille with Child Services. Can I talk with you about a client of mine?"

Lucille explained Marcie and Todd's situation without specifically mentioning anything magical. She described Marcie as a single mother raising a cute but sometimes difficult child. Eric commented that he'd seen this situation numerous times in his work. He had worked with children for several years but had recently moved here and was now taking on new clients. Lucille explained that it might be difficult for Marcie and Todd to come to his office, but a home visit would provide better insight into their situation. Eric agreed to meet them that afternoon.

Nervously, Lucille called Marcie to let her know they would arrive around 1:00 p.m. Marcie sounded ecstatic at the news of their coming. Lucille cautioned her about having too high expectations.

"Yes, yes, of course," Marcie responded. "I'll be positive but not overjoyed."

After the call, Lucille tried to focus on other cases but kept wondering how this would work out. Being able to do magic was an amazing talent, but how could she express concern about Todd's power being used for good—or not at all?

At last, 12:30 rolled around. Lucille had just finished a chicken and cheese wrap and scarfed down the last donut with a splash of coffee when she saw Eric enter her office. He was about 5'10", thin, with premature balding and wisps of thin hair over the top. His pinched face matched his pinched voice, Lucille surmised. His off-the-rack suit and thin black tie completed the look. Lucille stood up and waved to him from her desk.

"Hi, Eric."

"Hello, Lucille. Nice to meet you." He held out his hand, and when Lucille grasped it for a handshake, she had the sensation of holding a cold fish.

They chatted for a few minutes. Eric was new to the area, having recently moved from Cincinnati. He hadn't really established a practice yet—he had an office but only a few clients. Lucille drove Eric to the Arrington neighborhood without incident. No tickets, no yelling or cursing. Lucille was on her best behavior. It was a quiet ride, but Lucille was concerned about how well Eric would get along with Todd. There was an old-time TV show called *What's My Line?* Lucille was certain Eric would stump the panel on being a child psychologist. He was not at all what she had pictured. But wasn't that the way of things? You hear people on the radio with beautiful voices only to find out they're not what you imagined. In Eric's case, his voice was a perfect match for his demeanor.

Lucille pulled onto Hastings Avenue, and halfway down the block, they reached the tall wooden fence.

"Wasn't there something in the news this morning about an explosion near here?" Eric asked. "That fence was in the video they showed this morning."

"I don't know. Could be." Lucille quietly responded. She wasn't in a hurry to tell Eric about Todd's ability, though she had used Marcie's words—*Todd is a very special kid.* Eric said he didn't want to know more so his assessment wouldn't be biased. He would determine if he needed to meet with Todd again after the initial interview.

Before getting out of the car, Lucille phoned Marcie to say they had arrived. Marcie was apparently eagerly waiting just inside the gate. The deadbolts slid back, and the gate opened before they reached it. Marcie was all smiles to see them, though she looked a little concerned after getting a closer look at Eric. Nevertheless, she showed them inside. Lucille wondered what Eric's reaction would be to the interior, but it was Lucille who had the most reaction.

"Marcie, you've done something with the foyer, the living room?" Lucille turned around to see that, while the room still looked like a medieval hall, it was definitely smaller. The fire still blazed in the fireplace but was much closer to the front door.

"Yes, I convinced Todd that it should be a little smaller." She half-smiled at Lucille, while Eric gazed around at the room.

"Quaint," Eric said. "Interesting decorations, and a nice touch with the two torches on the wall. Your house must be a hit on Halloween."

"Yeah, I'm sure it is, isn't it, Marcie?" Lucille stifled her amazement at Eric's comment.

Marcie nervously looked around, then smiled weakly. "Yes, it is." Actually, all the deadbolts were checked and in place early on Halloween, and no one was allowed in. The neighborhood families hadn't tried trick-or-treating at their house for years.

Marcie had a table with four chairs arranged so they could sit and talk, bringing Todd in when needed.

Pleasantries ensued, and Eric asked questions about Marcie, Todd, and their family. Lucille realized that, aside from her visit the previous day, she didn't know much about Marcie, other than the magic problem.

Marcie asked about his psychology credentials, how long he had been practicing, and so on. It turned out Eric had only been certified as a child psychologist a few years ago. Before that, he had tried marriage counseling, but after he and his wife separated, he decided it wasn't his best fit. He'd always liked psychology but had to find the right niche.

After a little more chit-chat, Eric asked if he could meet Todd. Both Marcie and Lucille looked concerned but knew it had to happen. Marcie called for Todd on the wall phone, and shortly after, Todd appeared. No flowers this time. Todd looked a little apprehensive but settled into the fourth chair. Lucille and Eric both said hi to him, and Marcie stepped in to explain that Lucille had brought Mr. Swan to sit and talk with them about how Todd was doing and what he liked.

As soon as Eric began to talk, Todd scrunched up his face. It wasn't easy for him to listen to Eric's nasal, pinched voice. After a few awkward moments, Eric suggested he and Todd go into another room where they could talk more freely.

Dread spread across Marcie's face, but she said, "Sure. You can use the little den room through that door. It's comfortable."

The room had been her husband's office, and Marcie had insisted Todd not change it.

Todd and Eric walked over to the doorway. Todd glanced back before the door shut.

Marcie was nervous. Lucille held out her hand and spoke quietly with her. Lucille tried to take Marcie's mind off Todd and Eric. For the next twenty minutes, they talked about Marcie's life before she got married and the early years of raising Todd. They became immersed in Marcie's personal life—graduating from high school and going to a small women's college.

Then there was a crunching noise from the room where Todd and Eric were. Instantly, Marcie reached for the multi-colored phone on the wall.

"Todd, is everything okay? I heard a noise that sounded like a bottle being crushed."

Todd responded, "We're okay, Mr. Swan busted his pencil." "Yes, we're okay," a strange voice added.

Not entirely relieved, Marcie sat back down. Lucille tried to divert Marcie's attention, talking about her social life since her husband passed. Apparently, Marcie had virtually no social life since then, barely leaving the house. Both she and her husband were only children, both sets of parents were gone, and the past three years had been lonely. Their conversation continued as time wore on.

Suddenly, Lucille realized an hour had passed with no sign of either Todd or Eric. Once again, Marcie called Todd. Another strange voice answered—was it a woman's voice? "Yes, we're almost done."

Marcie sat back down, wondering if she had imagined the woman's voice. Everything felt muddled. With a questioning look at Lucille, she rested her head on her arms at the table.

Five minutes later, the door opened, and Todd came out, smiling. "Erica is finishing up some notes." Todd smirked and sat at the table. "I'm hungry. Can I have something to eat?"

Marcie nodded silently. Suddenly, a grilled cheese sandwich and potato chips appeared on a paper plate.

Lucille hadn't heard the woman's voice on the phone, but Marcie's reaction, and now this smirking little kid—Erica? Something was wrong.

Just then, a voluptuous woman appeared from Rob's old office. She was young, tall, with long black hair, wearing a tight yellow dress that came to her knees with a modest neckline. Her deep blue eyes sparkled, and she smiled as she approached Marcie and Lucille. "We had quite the talk. I've made some notes and would like to share some things with you. But first, do you have a bathroom? I need one."

Both Marcie and Lucille stared, unable to speak. Todd grinned and spoke up. "I'll show you."

"No, you won't! I'll show her where it is," Marcie snapped. Had her eyes been lasers, Todd would've been toast. "You stay right here with Lucille." Slowly, Marcie got up and motioned for the woman to follow her.

Todd's grin vanished. Ducking his head, he began nibbling his sandwich. Lucille was speechless, watching the exchange in disbelief. She turned to Todd and whispered, "How did you do this? Where's Mr. Swan?"

Todd glanced at her and shrugged.

Marcie returned moments later, slamming her chair around and leveling her gaze at Todd. "What did you do to Mr. Swan?" Marcie was ready to chew through steel.

"I don't know. He was weird, and the way he talked was annoying. I thought about changing him into dad, but that didn't seem right. I considered a knight, but that didn't work either—too rough. He broke his pencil and the table, you know, with the armor. Then I thought about someone nice, someone I liked, and didn't sound funny. That's when I thought of her—Erica."

Todd squirmed, looking sheepish. When he said her name, he briefly grinned.

Lucille rolled her eyes. How were they going to fix this?

"You've got to change him back, Todd," Marcie said, through clenched teeth.

Todd looked up at her defiantly. "No. I like her. She's pretty."

"Todd, you have to change her back to Mr. Swan. It's not fair to him. No one will recognize him. Wait—does he know what you did to him?"

"I don't think so. I think I wiped out his memory. He remembered for a bit, but then I erased it."

The three of them were huddled around the table when Erica returned.

She sat down, smiling. "Aww, it's so nice to see family and friends communicating." After a brief awkward silence, she continued, "Todd, would you mind leaving us for a while? I need to talk with your mom and Lucille." Todd jumped up and ran into another room.

Silence.

Erica began, "Marcie, first of all, you have a beautiful, loving son. He was so nice. He gave me three or four hugs."

Lucille, not surprised, twisted aside. *That little boy's face is just the right height for a hug,* she thought.

Erica went on, "I did pick up that Todd seems lonely. Does he have any playmates?"

Marcie's face was unreadable. "No." "And he misses his dad?"

"Yes."

"And I felt that he was hiding something from me. Would you know what that might be?"

"No," Marcie remained stoic.

Lucille watched the exchange, wondering who would break first. "What about school?"

"I homeschool him." "What about friends?" "None."

"Why?"

"Because . . ."

"Hmmm, I'd like to see him again. I think I can help draw him out—and maybe help you too."

Aha. There it was. Marcie looked like she was going to explode. Lucille could see that Marcie was trying hard to hold it together. Erica didn't seem to notice. She turned to Lucille. "We should be leaving soon. I have a late appointment at my office."

"Excuse me for just a moment," Marcie said. "I need to speak to my son." She grabbed the wall phone. "Todd, where are you? I need to speak to you. It's very important. Yes, Erica would like to see you again." She forced a smile. "I'll be right back." Her voice couldn't hide the dark undertone.

Lucille couldn't hold it in any longer. "So, Erica, how are you feeling now? Earlier you mentioned an upset stomach. Do you need some antacids? I have some in my purse."

"I feel fine. I don't recall anything about a stomach issue, but I think I have some in my purse too." Erica looked around, glancing under the table.

"That's odd. I don't have my purse here. Didn't I bring it?" Lucille shrugged. "I don't recall you carrying one."

"I must've left it in my office. Good thing I didn't get stopped by the police—I wouldn't have had my driver's license." Erica giggled nervously, fidgeting while waiting for Marcie.

Marcie returned and didn't sit down. "So, Erica, you said you wanted to see Todd again. How soon?" She was clearly ready to usher Erica out.

"Well, today's Tuesday. Normally, I have weekly appointments, but I have Friday open. How about 1 p.m. again? Here?"

"Yes, that's fine. I'll mark it on the calendar. I know you must be in a hurry. Todd, come say goodbye."

Todd ran in, gave Erica a hug, and dashed out, calling goodbye over his shoulder.

"Aww, so sweet," cooed Erica.

Lucille thought, *Oh brother.* "Okay, Erica, let's go." Marcie practically ran to the door to let them out.

"Bye, Lucille. I'll call you later. Bye, Erica. So glad you could come on such short notice. See you Friday!"

The bright sunlight outside was a shock. Lucille, leading the way, carefully descended the short stairs to the sidewalk.

Behind her, she heard a tight nasal voice, "Boy, that sunlight is hard to take after being in that house."

Lucille turned around to see Eric walking behind her in a suit and tie. Stunned by the change, Lucille stumbled on the sidewalk. Marcie had stopped on the porch, ecstatic upon seeing Eric's return. She skipped down the steps, closing the gate and waving cheerfully.

Lucille's head was spinning from the day's events. She wasn't sure if she should drive. She had a much clearer understanding of Marcie's situation now.

"Are you okay, Lucille? You look tired."

"Eric, I'm tired. I just need to sit for a minute." She turned to him. "Are you okay?"

"I'm okay, though I feel a little off. I'll be fine." He glanced at his watch. "We should get moving."

The drive back to Lucille's office was uneventful and quiet. Lucille asked if he needed anything. He declined, heading to his car with a "See you Friday."

Wait. Did I agree to come back to Marcie's on Friday? If Marcie wants it, I'll be there. This magic stuff is amazing. Lucille couldn't imagine Marcie's life—now there's a new wrinkle. Who would be there, Eric or Erica?

Lucille barely sat down in her chair when the receptionist called her name. "What's up, Marcie? Actually, I was going to call you. What happened back there? What did you say to Todd?"

"Well, what Erica said about Todd was pretty much what I had thought about Todd and his father, and the lack of friends. But I couldn't let Erica just walk out without understanding what was happening to her. Todd was so stubborn and defiant. He's never been like this. So this is what we settled on: as long as Eric isn't hurt by it, when Eric comes here, he'll be Erica. As soon as he leaves, he'll be Eric again. That's the only way I see this working. Todd will enjoy seeing Erica, but not Eric."

"Well, beyond that, Erica seems to understand Todd, but also, Erica is Todd's eye candy."

"Yes, I know," moaned Marcie.

The plan was set. Lucille didn't talk with Marcie for the next two days. Despite that, Lucille had a difficult time focusing on her other cases. Whenever there was a lull in activity at work or as she was home for the evening, her mind kept straying back to Eric/Erica and Marcie and Todd. As Todd became a teenager,

Lucille could see all kinds of complications developing. Would he become stronger with his magic abilities? While she knew Todd wasn't her kid, still, she felt some responsibility. Restless nights and bad dreams plagued her until Friday morning.

When Lucille arrived at work the next day, she'd already had two coffee shop coffees and immediately pounced on another cup. No caffeine headache would get to her today. The box of donuts on her desk was empty. She glared around the office. Someone had stolen the last two donuts. St. Johnny was back at his desk, but she knew he didn't do it. He'd jump a foot if she said hello to him. Well, she'd find out eventually. Fortunately, she had a spare in the bottom drawer. She pulled the box out and tore it open. She justified her donut fetish as a reward for a hard-working woman like her. Anyone disagreeing would see a cane swinging toward them.

The morning otherwise was uneventful. Lucille got some paperwork out of the way. When she looked up at the clock, it was noon. Time for another donut and coffee, she thought. There was a salad in the fridge, but it didn't look appetizing to her. Maybe someone else would eat it, she thought hopefully.

Eric arrived a little early. He told Lucille she didn't have to come with him, especially since she seemed to be busy. He would manage all right with Todd. Lucille said it was fine, and the time with Marcie would help them get to know each other better—better to help her and Todd (and she wasn't about to miss out on this visit for the world).

They traded some small talk on the way to Marcie's house. Eric was a late bloomer in psychology. He had graduated from college with an education degree, but teaching never seemed to work for him. He liked being around kids, but he just wasn't good at teaching. After three years of it, he decided to go back to school for a psychology degree and eventually opened a practice as a marriage counselor. He got married to a very nice woman, but after a couple of years, they just sort of lost interest in each other and amicably separated. So here he was now, working as a child psychologist. His nasal voice had been difficult for Lucille to listen to, but she made it.

For Lucille's part, she had been involved in the city's child services right out of college, which was a number of years ago. She had been married, but her husband had died. They had two kids, a boy and a girl. And now, she was a grandmother to three grandkids, all too far away to visit regularly. Thinking about her family was one of the few times she wasn't grumpy, bossy, or snarly. She was starting to feel emotionally down when they arrived at Marcie's. It was just 1 p.m.

Feeling the building apprehension, Lucille quickly forgot about her family as she walked around the front of the car while Eric was getting out. The gate was already open, with Marcie waiting for them. She looked nervous, her half-smile betraying it.

"Hi, good morning!" Marcie called out. She was dressed in her usual buttoned-down, untucked shirt and slacks, with pink shoes. "Oh, wait, it's afternoon, isn't it? Are you hungry? I could make some sandwiches."

"It's okay, Marcie. Speaking for the both of us, we don't need anything. Relax. Although, some of that lemonade you made really tasted good," responded Lucille.

"Yeah," chimed in Eric.

"Todd made it for me. I'll see if any of it's left."

They climbed the steps, Marcie holding open the door. Eric entered first, saw Todd standing in the front room, and called out, "Hi, Todd. How are you doing?" The first part of his question was in a masculine voice, the latter half in a feminine voice. As expected—hoped for—Eric became Erica as she entered the house. This time, she was wearing a tight red dress with a low neckline.

Todd, smiling broadly, came running up to Erica to give her a big hug. "Aw, this is so nice, Todd. I'm happy to see you too."

Marcie quickly came around to face Erica, noticed the low neckline, and turned to Todd with a look that said, "If you don't fix that neckline, I will spear you with a thunderbolt." Todd got the message, and with a blink, the neckline readjusted to something more modest. Erica didn't seem to notice.

Lucille, coming in last, missed the opening drama, but was still reeling over how magic worked. How did it work?

Lucille and Erica sat at the table where they had been last time, while Marcie told Todd he was helping to bring lemonade for everyone.

While they waited, Erica looked around the large foyer with the wall torches. "Very interesting how Marcie has decorated her home," Erica commented. "The torches really add atmosphere, and that fireplace . . . I'd love to sit on the floor in front of it."

Uh-huh, and Todd would love sitting up close beside you, thought Lucille. Lucille had another thought, an experiment, and said to Erica, "Have you ever been married?"

"No, never. I did have a close relationship, but it didn't work out. I thought I had told you this. Oh, well." Erica turned back to the fireplace.

Lucille stewed as she contemplated her next question. "Have you always been a child psychologist? Did you ever try being a marriage counselor?"

Erica wrinkled her face. "No, I never worked as a marriage counselor. I don't think I would be very good at it. I've always been a child psychologist, though once I thought about teaching. But having to make up lesson plans and dealing with unruly kids didn't sound good to me."

Not the same, but very close, thought Lucille.

Just then, Marcie and Todd came back with lemonade for everyone and a plate of oatmeal-raisin-nut cookies—Todd's favorite. More small talk ensued, then Erica leaned back. "Well, Todd, shall we go talk?" Erica smiled at him, and Todd almost jumped out of his chair. "Can we use your husband's office again? It's a very comfortable room." Marcie nodded, and the two of them left.

Once the room's door closed, Lucille whispered to Marcie, "Well?"

Marcie was quivering like a bowl of jelly. Lucille couldn't tell if she was nervous, happy, or excited. "Relax, Marcie."

Marcie gulped some of her lemonade. She took a deep breath. "I think it's working out the best we could have hoped for. Todd is getting some therapy that he really needed. Since Tuesday, he's been a different kid—acting happier than before Erica and not doing stupid magic things. He actually sat down and drew pictures on paper, rather than having them magically appear. Of course, the pictures were of Erica, but the point is, he didn't use magic."

Then Marcie turned serious. "Do you think this is ethical? Turning Eric into Erica? I mean, would Eric really agree to do something like this? It's like we're lying to him. But . . . but would he believe us if we told him what was happening?"

Given the current social climate, Lucille wasn't sure. Though, she had a hunch that Eric wouldn't like the back-and-forth transformations.

"I don't know. This has been so far around the corner for me that I can't properly figure it out. It's probably not ethical, but if Eric doesn't know, and he isn't physically harmed, does it matter? Ummm, I'm getting one of my headaches back. I'd better go for the aspirin. This feels like it's going to be a doozie." She reached for her purse to dig out the bottle.

"Oh, I nearly forgot." Marcie pulled a couple of photographs out of her shirt pocket and handed them to Lucille. "These two photos were lying out with some other papers that Todd had been looking at. I don't know how he found them." Lucille squinted at them. "Erica?"

"No," Marcie continued, "this woman was a distant cousin of my husband. She was a clothing model. She visited several years ago and left these photos. I wondered where he got the idea for Erica's appearance." The woman in the photos looked almost exactly like Erica, including the yellow dress from Tuesday.

From there, Marcie and Lucille talked on about a number of things, but Lucille kept steering Marcie back to talking more about herself. Since Tuesday, she had started questioning herself about her living arrangements with Todd, her lack of adult interactions, and how lonely she really was. Todd was a handful, keeping him from harming himself or anyone else. Homeschooling had been a problem at first, but Todd was eager to learn, and it gave him an outlet for his curiosity. Marcie had an arm's length of Todd stories, if anyone asked.

It was nearly 2:30 when Todd and Erica emerged from the office. Once again, Todd was smiling as well as Erica.

"Todd, why don't you run off? It's time for the grown-ups to talk." "Sure." Todd trotted off into another room.

"I know you must get tired of hearing this, Marcie, but Todd is such a wonderful child. I never get tired of getting hugs. Today, we talked about hobbies, and he showed me some card tricks that he knew. He's very good with them, always guessing the right card. Todd is such a loving—"

"Yeah, yeah, Todd is a lovely little boy that gives a thousand hugs," barked Lucille.

Erica gave Lucille a sideways glance and continued.

"One thing really apparent is that he needs a father figure. Is there anyone filling in that role now?" Erica looked directly at Marcie. Marcie shook her head no. Erica went on, "He's a very curious boy, and I think he would like to venture out of the house more."

Marcie spoke up defensively about how difficult things had been after her husband died and how they had somehow become hermits. Marcie had even arranged to have groceries delivered. Amazon was a godsend.

The three of them finished talking about possible ways to open up more to the outside world, mostly coming from Erica. Marcie and Lucille mostly nodded. Erica felt she was making progress with Todd and asked about seeing him again the next week. Would they like to come to her office? Marcie deferred the suggestion and asked to continue meeting at their house. Okay, they would meet at Marcie's home the following Wednesday at 1 p.m.

Eric/Erica came back the following two weeks. Both times Erica was wearing her red dress, and Todd enthusiastically greeted her. After the meetings, Erica talked with Marcie about her progress with Todd. Marcie was pleased with her comments.

Lucille continued with her work and nearly forgot about Eric/Erica. She was engrossed in several cases, and while she checked in with Marcie occasionally, it wasn't a detailed conversation. One thing Lucille did detect was that Marcie was a little melancholy. When Lucille asked, Marcie brushed it off.

At Marcie's house, things were a little different. While Todd liked seeing Erica, conversations with her had made him think more about his father. Todd began to crave more attention from a father figure. But Erica's last visit, Todd quietly observed his mother standing in front of her bedroom mirror. It was obvious she was comparing herself to Erica, and while standing there, she quietly talked to herself. Erica had touched a nerve with Marcie. She hadn't given it much thought, as she had been totally wrapped up dealing with Todd, but now it was really hitting home: she had no social life. Homeschooling Todd and exposing him to different ideas and knowledge was her social world. Feeling sorry for herself, she began to cry, sobbing quietly.

For the first time since his father died, Todd felt bad for his mother. He slipped away and went back to his room, filled with all sorts of odd things. Laying on his bed, he thought hard about how he could help his mother. It was going to be a few days before Erica would be back. It gave him plenty of time to think.

As usual, Eric pulled up, got out of his car, and Marcie greeted him at the gate. They walked up to the front door, and Erica stepped into the foyer. Todd seemed happy enough to see her, but he seemed a little distant compared to previous visits. Marcie waited patiently for Erica and Todd to talk in the office. Todd came out in just under an hour, smiling, and said Eric would come out in a minute. Marcie sat at the table with a couple of snacks. She looked up and saw a man—*Eric?*—walking out of the office. But this version of Eric was probably six feet tall and looking athletic. He wore a short-sleeved shirt and nice slacks. His hair was thick and dark brown in color. Clean-shaven and looking handsome. Marcie gawked at seeing him, expecting to see Erica. Without saying anything, she looked at Todd, whose smile gave way to a grin.

Eric came over, sat down at the table, and related his observations about Todd. Marcie could hardly keep her mind on the conversation because she was so distracted by Eric. First of all, the transition from Erica to this new Eric took her breath away. While annoyed with Erica on several points, she had grown to like her because Erica seemed to have good insights into Todd and his behaviors. But now, this new Eric—well, she felt tingly all over.

Finally, after discussing Todd, Eric asked if Marcie would like to continue his meetings with Todd, saying he felt Todd was doing better. Without hesitation, Marcie thought it would be good to have at least one more session. They made the appointment for the following week. Once outside the house, the new Eric resumed being the old Eric.

After Eric left, she pulled Todd close. "Why did you make a new Eric?" "Well, Erica was really cool and pretty. But I thought maybe you'd like someone who made you feel good."

Marcie nodded and hugged Todd. "Ach, you're strangling me," he laughed.

Over the years, Marcie had developed a daily routine: breakfast, homeschooling at 10:00 a.m., usually finishing by 1 or 1:30 p.m. Afterward came lunch and some playtime. Marcie had strict rules about what playtime meant—no destruction of property or harm to others. Whatever Todd created or altered had to be returned to its original state by 6:00 p.m., dinnertime. This was the part of the day that drove her the craziest. Often, Todd's idea of fun was vastly different from hers, which led to the day there was an elephant in the living room. Thankfully, there wasn't a basement.

Earlier in her life, Marcie had briefly considered going to art school. But she chose family life instead, using her doodles and sketches to help teach Todd. She had some of her drawings displayed on various walls of the house. Todd liked them, though for Marcie, they were reminders of what might have been. She missed her husband. At one point, Todd had asked if he should make a new dad, Rob. She told him no, that it wasn't a good idea. While she loved Rob, he was gone, and recreating him didn't feel right. As magically talented as Todd was, he wasn't God. But over the past three weeks, the loneliness had become unbearable, and the new Eric stirred up many emotions.

Absently, she took out her art pad and began doodling circles and swirls while sitting at her dressing table. She glanced up at her mirror and sketched the outline of her face and figure. She wondered how she might look with a smaller nose, a broader smile, or a more striking figure. Her mind raced with "what-ifs," and her doodles became more intense. She added lines, erased others, and shaded in different places. After a while, she paused, holding the drawing up to compare it with her reflection in the mirror. Her hand began to tremble. She set the pad down, got up quickly, and went to check on Todd. It was nearly suppertime, and although Todd had the ability to create a meal out of thin air, she preferred the traditional way of preparing food.

Over the years, Marcie had grown accustomed to restless nights, worrying about how to handle Todd. But tonight, after supper, she lay in bed, wondering about herself and what the future held. Unable to sleep, she slipped out of bed earlier than usual and picked up the drawing pad again. She studied her drawing, set the pad down, and began preparing for the next day. Breakfast came and went, and they started their schoolwork at ten, but Marcie struggled to concentrate. Todd sensed her distraction and didn't focus either. By noon, Marcie was so frustrated, she told Todd they were done for the day. They'd have an early lunch, and she allowed Todd to make his favorite—partially burnt grilled cheese sandwiches with runny cheese. He didn't like tomato soup like Marcie did, so while she enjoyed her soup and sandwich, Todd had three sandwiches and milk.

As they finished their meal, Marcie picked up the drawing pad and held it up in front of Todd. "What do you think of this picture?"

"Neat. It's neat, I guess. Is that you?" He turned to compare the drawing with his mother.

"Well, yes and no. Let me ask you, can you make me look like this?" Her arm began to shake with nervousness.

"Yeah, I can do that. But why?"

"Because I've reached a point where I need to be a new me."
"But you look okay to me. You're my mother."

"Yes, I know. But sometimes a person needs to reinvent themselves. When you're older, you'll understand. Can you do it now?" *Before I lose my nerve?* she thought.

Todd held the drawing in front of him, blinked, then set it down. He looked at Marcie. "You were pretty before, Mom, but now you're prettier." He smiled, and they hugged.

She kissed him on the forehead, sniffled back tears. "Thank you, sweetie. Now go play." As touching as the moment was, she couldn't wait to look in the mirror in her bedroom. She closed the door, undressed, and examined herself. Her nose was smaller, not so wide. Her smile was broader, showing off her white teeth. And she now had cheekbones! Otherwise, she looked like her old self, but better. Her brown hair had taken on an auburn hue. She stood back and checked her figure. Yes, there was more sizzle—nothing like Erica, but more than the old Marcie. And she was a couple of inches taller. *Nice work, Todd.* Satisfied, Marcie pulled the covers back and lay down. She buried herself in the blankets, half-laughing, half-crying, and soon fell asleep.

She didn't wake up until 6:45 p.m., past suppertime. Quickly, she dressed and went to the kitchen. Todd had already eaten, mostly chicken tenders and applesauce. After a quick snack, Marcie sat at her desktop, searching for new clothes and accessories. It was only three days until the new Eric would arrive.

For a while, things felt relatively normal. Lucille continued her work. She figured out who had taken her donuts and gave them an earful. A new box of donuts appeared on her desk the following day. She kept her grumpy demeanor, and somehow, her office seemed to run more smoothly because of it. She hadn't spoken to Marcie since Erica's second visit, but out of curiosity, Lucille decided to call her and check in.

"Hi, Marcie. I'm just checking in. How are you doing?"

"Everything is going really well. Todd's doing great. He's cut back on his magical shenanigans and is spending more time with me, aside from schoolwork," Marcie said, sounding upbeat and happy.

"Sounds like Erica is still working with Todd?" Lucille asked. "Oh, Lucille, Erica's gone. She's been replaced with a new Eric." "Tell me more," Lucille said, curious about the change.

"Well, it was Todd's idea. I guess he noticed that I didn't have many people to talk to, so he said goodbye to Erica and brought in a new Eric. Just like that! Listen, why don't you come by tomorrow? Eric's coming at one, and you can see for yourself."

"Uh, okay. I'll check my schedule. I think I can make it." "Great, see you tomorrow."

Lucille hung up and stared at her phone, snorting in disbelief. *Something's going on here,* she thought. While it was Marcie's voice, her demeanor had changed—she sounded full of life and energy, not the hesitant and polite Marcie Lucille had first met. She was looking forward to seeing this "new" Eric the next day.

The next day, Lucille arrived before 1:00 p.m., eager to see what was going on. Something felt off. Since she was early, she had to wait for Marcie to let her in the gate. She heard the deadbolts slide and the gate creak open.

Lucille started walking through but stopped in her tracks. "Marcie?" Marcie stood there, beaming with her new smile. Lucille looked her up and down. Marcie was still wearing her button-down shirt and jeans, along with her pink running shoes, but now her shirt was a vibrant paisley pattern instead of bland plaids. There was more to her—she even looked . . . sexy. Marcie had once been shorter than Lucille, but now they were eye to eye. Lucille stared in awe. Marcie's hair, her face—this wasn't just makeup.

"How . . . ?" Lucille asked, baffled.

"Todd. I gave him a drawing of a new me, and here I am!" Marcie twirled around with her arms outstretched.

"Why? Does this have something to do with the 'new' Eric?" "Yes!"

Just then, Eric pulled up to the curb behind Lucille's car. He got out and walked toward them. "Hi, Lucille, Marcie." He paused. "You look different, Marcie. Did you dye your hair?" he asked in his nasal voice.

Marcie looked a little deflated by his comment but quickly ushered them toward the house. Lucille wondered how Eric would look inside. It didn't take long. Lucille stepped through the front door first, then turned to watch Eric enter. She blinked—Eric had transformed from the thin, slightly balding, nasal-voiced man into a taller athletic-looking version with thick brown hair and a well-dressed appearance. It all became clear to Lucille now—Marcie had the hots for Eric!

Todd greeted them, and Lucille noticed that his smile was different from the one he had with Erica. *Todd really likes this new Eric,* she thought.

Without hesitation, Eric suggested having another session with Todd. He was a little pressed for time since he had a meeting with a realtor later in the afternoon. So off they went to the office.

Marcie's excitement dimmed when she overheard Eric mention the realtor. "What does that mean?" she asked rhetorically, turning to Lucille.

"Search me," Lucille replied. "Maybe he's looking for a new house?"

Marcie frowned but then began discussing her "new" self with Lucille.

Lucille listened and understood, and it was lucky for Marcie that Todd was able to help; otherwise, her new look would have cost her thousands. After reflecting on Marcie's new body, Lucille wondered about herself having a new body. Naw, she preferred being pudgy and grumpy.

Todd and Eric returned about forty-five minutes later. Todd went off to give the adults space to talk. Eric shared that Todd was doing well and didn't think he'd need more sessions, which was good because Eric had decided to move out of state. He wasn't comfortable in Indiana and longed to be in one of the western states. That was what the meeting with the realtor had been about—selling his house. He wasn't sure where he'd relocate to yet, but he'd figure it out.

Marcie's heart sank with the news. She kept a brave face. Eric's positive assessment of Todd reassured her, but it also meant no more meetings with Eric. Lucille kept an eye on Marcie while Eric spoke, feeling bad for her. Just as Marcie's life was taking a turn for the better, this new development felt like a bump in the road.

Eric checked his watch. "Oops, it's getting late. Sorry, I've got to meet my realtor." He stood up. "It's been nice getting to know you and Todd, Marcie. Lucille, I'll drop off a copy of my notes for you. Thanks for your help."

As Eric moved toward the door, he turned and added, "Oh, I almost forgot to say—Marcie, you really look nice today." He smiled, and she smiled back, looking appropriately modest.

"Oh, wait a second, Eric, can I get a picture of you and Todd before you leave? You've been a big help."

"Okay, but quickly," Eric said, already stepping down the sidewalk. "Todd, come here! I want to take a photo of you and Eric," Marcie called out. She knew he was probably in the "listening to the adults talk" range. He appeared out of nowhere, ran out the door, then hesitated when he saw Eric had returned to his old self. He turned back to Marcie, mouthing, *What?*

"Go on, get out there," she scolded him.

He joined Eric, who placed a hand on Todd's shoulder. Todd grimaced, but Marcie quickly snapped the picture. "Bye, thank you." She waved. Eric waved back and left. Marcie called Todd back into the house and went to close the gate. She'd learned long ago that Todd, eager to see the world outside, would slip out if given the chance. *Old habits are hard to break,* she thought.

Later that evening, Eric called Marcie. In his nasal, pinched voice, he asked if she'd like to have dinner the following night. He had met with his realtor, and although he was still making plans to move, he thought it would be nice to get together. Marcie quickly responded that she'd like to, but would prefer if he came to dinner at her place with her and Todd, instead of going out. It would take time for both her and Todd to adjust to venturing out more. Eric agreed, and they set the time for 7:00 the next night.

Marcie went to bed excited and woke up the next morning still excited, though a bit apprehensive. When Todd got up, Marcie asked him to confirm that Eric would indeed be the handsome Eric when he arrived. He assured her he would be.

The afternoon seemed to drag on forever as Marcie anticipated the evening. Suddenly, it was 6:00. She prepared Todd's favorite chicken-broccoli-cheese casserole and dressed in her new clothes—new versions of slacks and shirts. She was still getting used to wearing a dress. Eric arrived at 7:00, and Marcie greeted him at the gate. He'd brought a bottle of wine and a mechanical dog for Todd. As soon as Eric stepped across the threshold, he became the new Eric, and Marcie's smile grew even wider. The dinner went well. Marcie's casserole was a hit, and Todd had magically decorated the table with two small vases of flowers at Marcie's request. Marcie had also sternly requested that there be no magic while Eric was present. The conversation was occasionally awkward, but overall, the evening went well. So well, in fact, that before leaving, Eric asked if she'd have dinner with him again. She agreed to meet on Saturday night, but wanted to host again at her place.

The next day, Thursday, Marcie called Lucille again and asked if she could come to the house. Lucille checked her schedule, saw she had a free slot, and agreed. Marcie prepared a small healthy meal—no donuts this time. When Lucille arrived, Marcie led her to the kitchen table. Lucille sniffed at the cut-up fruit and veggies, eating a few bites, but the main reason Marcie had invited her over was to talk about Eric—how she felt about the previous night and her desire to see him again to see where things might go. She had a good feeling about him, but she knew there was a problem looming: they could only spend time together at her house. No dining out, no movies in theaters, and so on. How could she explain that Eric magically transformed every time he came over? Lucille agreed that this would be a challenge, but unless Eric was totally comfortable with only visiting her house, Marcie would eventually have to break it to him. Who knew how he'd react?

"There are probably very few people, if any in history, who would have to deal with something like this. Marcie, if you take my advice, be upfront with Eric. It's not going to be easy, but if you think he likes you, you've got to give him the chance to express it. From all my years of living, I've found the best way to deal with a problem is to face it head-on. It may be painful, but whatever it is, it'll be done, and you won't have to agonize over it. You don't have a choice—you've got to take a chance."

Marcie shrugged and sighed. "Yes, you're right, but how do I do this?" "How about," Lucille suggested with a grin, "Eric, you know, you look really good in a dress."

Marcie grabbed a piece of broccoli and tossed it at Lucille, who burst out laughing. It took a while for Lucille to regain her composure.

"I don't know, Marcie, but I'm sure you'll figure it out. I've gotta run. Thanks for the no-donut lunch," Lucille said, her tone dripping with sarcasm. She swung her cane and made her way to the front door. On one of the walls outside the kitchen, there was a framed picture of a white cat, the plaque beneath it reading "Kitty Kat." Lucille nodded to the cat as she continued toward the door.

Marcie followed Lucille out to the gate and waved goodbye. She was not looking forward to Saturday. She had two days to figure out what to say.

Saturday evening arrived quickly, and Marcie still didn't have a plan for how to tell Eric about Todd's magical abilities and what he did with them. She worried this could be a breaking point in her and Eric's relationship, so she decided to wear a dress after all. She needed to tip the odds in her favor. It was a simple fuchsia V-neck dress—hopefully just right. Her new figure looked great in it. After a moment's hesitation, she added a touch of perfume from a nearly full bottle, her fingers trembling slightly. When Todd saw her, he did a double take.

"Wow, Mother! What are you wearing?" he asked, eyes wide.

Marcie realized Todd probably hadn't seen her in a dress in nearly three years. She blushed. "It's a dress, Todd. You know, like Erica wore, and Lucille." She knew he was teasing, and his playful comment made her laugh—a perfect tension reliever.

Eric arrived dressed in his usual suit and tie, and Marcie greeted him at the gate. He immediately noticed her new look and complimented her on it. As they entered, the new Eric appeared and shook hands with Todd. When asked if he was hungry, Eric said yes, everything smelled great—including her. Marcie smiled at the compliment and led him to the kitchen for dinner.

Dinner was pleasant, with good conversation among the three of them, though Marcie felt a bit anxious, which occasionally showed in her voice. After the meal, they cleaned up together, with Eric helping Marcie load the dishes into the dishwasher. Usually, Todd cleaned the plates magically, but Marcie had again told him no magic while Eric was there. Once the cleanup was finished, Marcie poured wine for herself and Eric, and they moved to the living room.

"Nice cat," Eric remarked, nodding toward the picture of Kitty Kat. They settled onto the luxurious sofa (courtesy of Todd) and placed their wine glasses on the coffee table.

Marcie took a moment to thank Eric for his attention to Todd. She felt both she and Todd had benefited from the sessions.

"Yes, I'm glad it worked out well for him," Eric replied, "and it gave me a chance to learn more about you."

After a brief pause, Eric continued, "There's something odd in my notes, though—those handwritten ones I gave Lucille a typed copy of, by the way. She's a pistol. I wouldn't want to get on her bad side."

"I agree." Marcie laughed softly. "But she's become a friend to me." She turned serious. "You said you found a problem?"

"Oh, yes. As I was going through the notes, I noticed something strange. It looks like two, maybe three people wrote them. The handwriting changes on different pages. Some of it looks like a woman's handwriting, you know, a little swirly, while mine is blockier. Some of the writing looks like mine but . . . different. I remember writing all of it, but I must have been really tired when I wrote some of it."

Marcie's heart started pounding, a mix of guilt, hopeful anticipation, and understanding. This was her opening. Did she have the courage to go through with it?

"Eric, I want to thank you again for working with Todd and me. But there's probably one thing you aren't aware of," she said.

Eric raised an eyebrow. "Oh? Your hands are trembling. Nervous about something? You might want to set your glass down before you spill it."

Marcie took a deep breath and called, "Todd, please come here." When he didn't come immediately, she picked up the multi-colored phone on the wall and spoke into it. "Todd, please come to the living room." She turned to Eric. "Sometimes he's engrossed in his playroom. I can solve your handwriting problem, but first, you need to see something."

Todd eventually appeared in the living room, a questioning look on his face. "What?"

"It's time to show one of your talents to Eric. Can you do something simple?"

Todd hesitated. "You mean, now?"

Marcie nodded while Eric looked on, mystified. "Can you give me a pencil?" she asked.

Todd pulled out a small stubby #2 yellow pencil from his pocket.

Marcie raised an eyebrow. "Can I have a real pencil?"

Todd pulled out another short pencil. A little annoyed, Marcie said,

"Todd, give me a whole box of pencils."

With a smirk, Todd reached into his back pocket and pulled out a small box containing ten pencils. It could have easily fit in his pocket.

Marcie straightened up, glanced at Eric, and shot Todd a disapproving look. Eric, confused, watched the scene unfold. What special talent?

"Todd, please make a little bunny and put it on the table." Todd ran off, returning with a piece of notepaper, quickly drew a small bunny, and placed it on the table. He couldn't contain his smirk.

Marcie shot him a piercing look. "Now."

With a sigh and a quick hand gesture, Todd made the small bunny appear in his palm. It was white and sniffed around his hand. He gently placed it on the table. "Thank you," Marcie said, thinking, *It's about time, you little smart aleck.*

She turned to Eric, who was staring in confusion at the bunny moving around the coffee table.

"How did you do that? It's so small. So you're some kind of magician, boy, that's some trick. I remember the card tricks you showed me before. You're really good."

"Todd, the bunny's pretty small. Can you make it bigger?" Marcie asked.

Todd shrugged, and with a flick of his wrist, the bunny grew into a full-sized rabbit. It continued sniffing around, seemingly unaffected by its new size.

"Wow." Eric's voice was soft with awe. "How did you do that? You just made it a big rabbit. How?" His face was wide-eyed, and his mouth hung open. He reached out to touch the rabbit, which didn't mind. Again, he said, "How?"

Marcie took Eric's left hand and held it tightly. Softly, she said, "Eric, Todd can do magic—more than just card tricks. He can do anything he wants, but with my restrictions," she added quickly, shooting a quick glance at Todd.

Eric didn't respond, clearly stunned.

"Todd, do a few simple things. Nothing fancy," she instructed.

Todd stood still for a moment, then held out his hand, palm up. A medium-sized plastic ball appeared. He tossed it into the air, and it bounced once on the floor. On the second bounce, it transformed into three carrots that landed on the table. The rabbit immediately began nibbling on them.

Marcie had continued holding Eric's hand, but now he was squeezing it so hard it hurt. "Eric, are you okay?" she asked, growing worried. She didn't know how he would react to Todd's magical abilities, but at this moment, it seemed like she might need to calm him down. "Todd, honey, please take the bunny and the carrots to your room. It's time for grown-ups to talk. Thank you." Todd picked up the rabbit, stuffed the remaining carrots in his pants pocket, and carried it away to his room.

Eric finally gasped, "How long has he been able to do this? I . . . I don't understand."

Calmly, Marcie responded, "We first noticed Todd's ability when he was about six months old. If toys or his binky were out of reach, he would look at them, and they would slide across the floor or bed to him. Later, when he got hungry and we didn't have food right away, a cookie would just appear. Rob, my husband, and I tried asking the pediatrician about it, but he just brushed it off, saying babies can't do those things, and we probably just weren't paying close enough attention.

"At first, things were okay, but as Todd got older, it became more complicated dealing with him and his abilities. He had his kitty that he brought to life, and that's when things really started getting strange. Rob and I tried to rein him in on his magic. We succeeded somewhat, convincing Todd that magic was only for good things—not to hurt people or mess with their property."

Spellbound, Eric nodded slowly. "Uh-huh."

"That's when we decided to put a fence around the yard to stop neighbors from complaining about strange things happening to their stuff. After Rob died, it became harder to handle Todd. He's a good boy—very loving and not a bad kid. You know that now. He's just a kid with exceptional abilities."

"Uh, yeah, Todd is a nice kid. I've grown to like him, but why didn't you bring this up earlier?"

"Why? Would you have believed me? And if it got out that Todd could do these magical things, who knows what would have happened? He'd have been treated like some kind of monster, and who knows where he would have ended up? The older he gets, the stronger he seems to get." She paused. "That's why we spent so much time trying to teach him to be nice, to respect us, to do what we told him. But even then, it was becoming too much for me to handle. I needed help, and that's where Lucille and you came in."

Marcie fell silent, and they sat in uneasy stillness for a few minutes. It was clear Eric was trying to process everything, turning his head and muttering to himself as if debating internally. Marcie drained the last of her wine in a single gulp.

"Okay, just so I have this straight," Eric began, "Todd's been able to do magic stuff since he was about six months old? He can make things appear out of nowhere? And he's getting better, stronger, as he gets older?"

Marcie nodded.

"So I mentioned earlier that I had a problem with some differences in handwriting in my notes. Why do I feel so anxious about this now?"

Marcie's nerves were starting to show more. Her hands trembled, and her voice wavered.

"Well, the first time you came—uh . . ." Lucille's advice about tackling problems head-on came to mind. "Well, the first time you came here to talk with Todd, he didn't like . . . you," she said, her voice shaking. "But you were the first man he'd been around since his father passed away—about three years ago." She paused, then, emboldened, continued, "But, well, you were different then than you are now." She grimaced as the words left her lips.

They had been sitting side by side, but now she turned to face him. "Eric, you're a different man from when you first came here." There. She said it.

Eric scowled. "What do you mean by 'different'?"

Marcie reached for an envelope on the end table beside her, one she had placed there in anticipation of this moment. Pulling out a photo, she held it for a moment before speaking. "Do you remember a few days ago when I took a picture of you and Todd, out here on the front sidewalk? Here it is." Her hands trembled again.

Eric took the photo and stared at it. "What is this? Who's that standing next to Todd?"

"You."

His brows knitted, and he looked up at Marcie, seeking an explanation.

"Todd has a spell on the house. Whenever you come in, you come through the gate looking like you in the photo, but once you step through the front door, you become . . . you, as you are now." Marcie cringed. She had no idea how he would react to this.

"Let me get this straight. When I come through your door, I look like I do now?"

"Yes."

"So when I leave here, I'll go back to looking like me in the photo?" "Yes."

"Why?"

"So you'll look like the *you* other people know." Another cringe moment.

"Do you have a mirror?"

"In the bathroom, around the—"

"Yeah, I know where it is. I'll be right back."

Eric stood and walked around to the left, disappearing through the doorway. Marcie sat uneasily on the couch, her trembling hands fidgeting with the hem of her dress. After a couple of minutes, Eric returned, sat down on the couch with some space between them, and tossed the photo onto the coffee table.

"So when I'm here, I look like this athletic guy with a nice head of hair, and when I leave, I go back to being this thin, balding guy?"

"Yes, but you're still the same person inside." Her voice sounded hopeful, though uncertain.

"And Todd did this to me?"

"Yes"

"How come I don't remember this happening?"

"That's part of the spell. It was a compromise."

"Compromise? What compromise?"

"I told you that when you first came here, Todd didn't like you. You didn't fit his image of his father, so he changed your appearance."

"To how I look now?"

"No, at first he thought of changing you to look like Rob, but then decided that wasn't right. We had talked about it before—about how it wouldn't be right to recreate Rob. So he changed you into a knight . . . with armor. But he didn't like that either."

"So?"

Marcie felt her hands trembling again, so she reached for the other photograph in the envelope. She hesitated for a moment, then held it close to her chest before offering it to Eric. "This photo isn't of you, but it was Todd's inspiration for your appearance." Slowly, she handed it over. It was the photo of Rob's cousin, the clothing model.

Eric glanced briefly at Marcie before taking the photo. He studied it, his face unreadable. After several long seconds, he slowly laid it on the table. The silence stretched between them, becoming unbearable. Marcie couldn't stand it.

"Todd said her name was Erica."

That was all it took. Eric burst out laughing. He laughed so hard his face turned red, and he slid down the couch. It took a while for him to calm down, gasping for breath between chuckles. "That explains the handwriting in my notes," he said, barely able to catch his breath before laughing again. Marcie just watched him, unsure of what to do.

"Erica? What a babe! He's nearly twelve, but the hormones are already working. I bet he liked to hug her."

"Yes, he did."

"Is that it, or is there more?"

Marcie hesitated for a moment before answering. "Well, Todd and I had an argument about how he had changed you into Erica. At first, he didn't want to change you back to your old self. We finally worked out a deal where you'd be your old self until you walked into our house. Then you'd change into what Todd wanted. It's the first time Todd's ever argued with me about his magic."

"Well, that explains some of the language in my notes," Eric muttered. "So he wanted me to be Erica. But how is it I look like a dude now?"

"At first, I needed help dealing with Todd, and I didn't think much beyond that. After your first visit, when Erica appeared, I was hoping to get advice on handling him. But I didn't want people to know about his magic, except for Lucille. She's been a big help to me as well. After the shock of seeing Erica . . . uh, you, sorry, I realized 'you'—Erica—had some insights into Todd that I hadn't considered before. I was encouraged to keep going with your sessions. And if I had to compromise with Todd, well, it was worth it to me."

"And what about me?" Eric asked, his tone turning more serious.

"That was a dilemma," Marcie admitted. "Lucille and I talked about whether it was a good or bad idea to let Todd keep changing you. We couldn't see that you were being hurt by it, and Todd worked it so you wouldn't remember who you were while you were here." Her voice faltered, and she felt the tears welling up. "We knew that sooner or later, we'd have to tell you." She struggled to hold herself together but was on the verge of sobbing.

Eric leaned over and gently hugged Marcie, offering some comfort as she started to calm down.

"So how did I, the dude, show up? A twelve-year-old nearing puberty would've probably kept Erica around." Eric's voice softened with curiosity.

Marcie wiped her eyes and continued, her voice shaky but more steady now. "You've done so much for us. After Erica showed up, I started questioning myself. I felt physically insecure with her here. For the first time, I realized I was lonely. I needed someone as much as Todd needed a father figure. Todd picked up on that, and well, here you are."

"What a neat kid. I'm impressed." Eric chuckled.

Marcie's eyes glistened again. "Oh, trust me, he was sad to see Erica go. He almost changed his mind, but here you are." Her voice broke, but she quickly added, "I love him."

They embraced for a while, Eric resting his head gently on hers. "So now what?" Eric asked softly.

"Well, eventually you'll leave and revert to old Eric. I drew a picture of how I wanted to look and showed it to Todd. He worked wonders on me. I'm not going back to the old Marcie."

"Yeah, I noticed a change right away," Eric said with a playful growl.

Marcie sat up and punched him lightly on the shoulder. "Ouch," he winced, laughing.

They continued talking about their identities. Eric picked up the photo of Todd and himself. "I've got a brother out there somewhere," he said thoughtfully. "We're not really close, and most of my other relatives are either dead or in nursing homes." He paused. "When I decided to move out of the city, I notified my few clients, told them I'd be unavailable, and directed them to other psychologists. Todd was my last one." He was getting to the point. "I like seeing myself as the new Eric. I've always felt physically inhibited. Glasses, balding, frail physique—it just didn't sit right with me. But this new body . . . it makes me feel at ease." He mimicked his old, nasal voice, and they both laughed.

"So how do we do this?" he asked.

"To do what?" Marcie replied, knowing exactly what he meant but wanting to make sure.

"To make this permanent." He swept his hand across his body.

"We need Todd . . . ," Marcie began, but before she could finish, Eric nudged her and nodded toward the door. Todd was quietly walking into the room. After putting the rabbit in his room, he had come back to settle into a bean bag chair, clearly eavesdropping.

"Todd, we need you to lift the house spell on Eric." Marcie said it simply, but Todd flashed a smile and said, "Sure." He waved his hand in front of Eric's face, and suddenly, old Eric was sitting on the couch.

Eric looked around, thoroughly confused. "What the—"

Marcie snapped around to Todd. "Todd, undo this! You know what I meant!"

Todd's laugh faded into a smirk. With another wave of his hand, new Eric reappeared on the couch. As Eric opened his mouth to speak, his voice came out high and squeaky, like he'd just inhaled helium. Todd burst out laughing, and even Marcie couldn't help but grin, though she quickly turned to Todd with a look that could kill.

"Todd, stop playing around." Her glare deepened.

With one more wave of his hand, new Eric was whole again.

"So this is how I'll look when I leave tonight?" Eric asked, a touch of disbelief in his voice. "No more changing back to old Eric? And no more dresses?"

Todd reassured him with a playful grin, "No more messing around." "Good," Eric said, relief flooding through him. "I was starting to change

my mind about you!"

Marcie glanced at the clock. It was getting late, and she had a strict bedtime for Todd, which was fast approaching.

"Todd, say good night to Eric and get to bed," Marcie said gently.

Todd quickly gave Eric a hug, though Eric had initially extended his hand for a handshake. The hug surprised both of them, but Todd turned and gave Marcie a hug as well. "I love you, Mother."

"I love you too," she replied, her voice filled with warmth.

Marcie and Eric continued talking about selling his house. The realtor had warned that the housing market wasn't doing well. It was a buyer's market, and it might take a while to sell. Marcie asked him where he wanted to move, but he was vague. "Just somewhere other than here," he said.

After a while, both of them were getting tired. Eric decided it was time to leave. Marcie walked him to the gate, and timidly, Eric approached the doorway. He held his breath and stepped onto the porch. Both of them were relieved when he didn't revert to his old self. They shared a kiss and a warm hug, ending the evening. Eric promised to call tomorrow and waved as his car pulled away from the curb. Marcie closed the gate and walked back to her house, lost in thought.

It took a long time to sell Eric's house. A month passed with only two people asking for a tour. An open house had just three visitors who wandered through the small early 1950s house with a modest yard and no remarkable features. The house mirrored Eric's mood when he first moved to town—unremarkable, but a place to start over.

Eric and Marcie continued dating, and now that Todd wasn't so preoccupied with magic tricks, they made occasional outings to parks and even went to the zoo. The zoo trip, however, ended abruptly when an alligator died under strange circumstances.

Another month passed, and by then, Eric had proposed to Marcie. She couldn't help but wonder what had taken him so long. Neither of them had many friends or relatives, so they decided on a small ceremony in Marcie's backyard. They asked a pastor to perform the ceremony, and Lucille agreed to be Marcie's bridesmaid. Eric had one acquaintance who would be his best man, and Lucille had a couple of office mates who knew Marcie through her. The wedding date was set for early October.

Both Eric and Marcie worked with Todd to conjure up suitable decorations, and to save money, Todd would also produce the wedding rings. Marcie and Eric picked out designs from a catalog and online. Todd took a surprising interest in the rings, even helping to select their design.

The wedding day went smoothly. Marcie, concerned that Todd might use the occasion for one of his magical surprises, asked him not to do anything disruptive. Todd agreed, though he did have one small idea that he thought they might like. A simple archway adorned with multi-colored ribbons and balloons added a festive touch. A small platform covered part of the yard where the arch rested. A lone sugar maple had started to turn colors, adding to the autumn ambience. One of Lucille's office mates played the recorded wedding songs, and Todd was set to be the ring bearer. Lucille, besides being Marcie's bridesmaid, was in charge of the photos. Unknown to most, Lucille liked to go out on weekends to photograph buildings, landscapes, and quirky scenes—her way of relieving stress.

The ceremony lasted only about twenty minutes. The pastor was warm and efficient, smoothly moving through the readings, vows, and "I dos." Todd delivered the rings on cue, placed on a satin pillow with tassels at each corner. When the pastor announced, "You may kiss the bride," Todd couldn't resist adding his own touch. He waved his hand, and hundreds of monarch butterflies swarmed up from two cages on either side of the arch. They flew over the couple before drifting southward. (As part of their homeschool curriculum, Marcie had taught Todd about the life cycle of monarchs and how their numbers were declining.)

Everyone hugged and thanked the pastor, and Todd, at Marcie's direction, provided a small luncheon. Marcie had a small bouquet of flowers, but instead of throwing it over her shoulder, she handed it directly to Lucille with a smile. "You're next, sweetie." Lucille accepted the bouquet, but as soon as Marcie turned away, Lucille set the bouquet on the plate of one of her unmarried officemates. She would have given it to St. Johnny, but he had a conflict and couldn't make it.

Eric had already moved his belongings into Marcie's house, so when everyone had left after the wedding, all three of them were finally able to relax. Eric and Marcie were curled up on the couch, sound asleep. Todd was holding a paperback book he had found some time ago—about knights, dragons, and magic—just the kind of book he loved. He flipped through the pages, read a little more, then fell asleep as well.

Though the wedding was over, there was still an air of anticipation. A week had passed, and Eric's house still hadn't sold, despite him agreeing to drop the price by a few thousand dollars. They had planned a honeymoon—a family trip—once the house was sold, but of course, they couldn't make reservations until that happened. Eric was reconsidering his psychology practice, though he still had his sights set on heading out west. Marcie, on the other hand, was still anxious about Todd. While things had improved with his magical escapades, it was hard to completely relax after so many years of watchful concern. But it was definitely easier now with two adults watching over him. They could take turns getting out of the house, which was a much-needed relief for Marcie. Overall, everyone was much happier than they had been before Lucille had called Eric. They were all looking forward to the future.

A few days later, Todd was playing in his room, which he had expanded to give him more space for kicking soccer balls around. Everything seemed fine until one of the soccer balls he kicked with extra force careened off the wall and unexpectedly hit him on the head, knocking him off his feet. He fell and hit his head on one of the metal legs of a nearby table. He was out cold. He lay there, bruised and bleeding. Fortunately, Marcie had just called him, and when he didn't respond, she started looking for him. She found him lying on the floor, panic rising in her chest. Terrified, she called Eric, and soon they were on their way to the ER.

After several hours of worry and tests, the doctors confirmed that Todd had suffered a concussion from hitting the table leg. They assured them that with rest, he'd be fine. "No kicking soccer balls for a week," the doctor warned. Relieved, they left the ER after about seven long hours. On the way home, Todd complained that something didn't feel right—like he was missing something in his head. His parents assured him they would keep an eye on him and told him that he'd feel better after more rest.

That evening, Todd realized what was missing. While lying in bed, he needed a tissue and tried to materialize one, but nothing happened. Surprised and alarmed, he tried to bring his ball to him magically, but again, nothing. The ball didn't move. He tried other things, but nothing responded to his will. A cold shiver of loss ran through him. He knew something was wrong. He quietly got out of bed and went to find Marcie and Eric. He shook Marcie awake and crawled into bed with her.

"I know why my head feels funny, Mother. I can't do magic anymore." Marcie, still half asleep, gently stroked his hair back, pulled him close, and laid back down.

The next morning, they woke to the sounds of Eric attempting to make breakfast. He wasn't doing too well. Marcie, still in her nightgown, and Todd, still in his pajamas, wandered into the kitchen and plopped down at the table. Marcie desperately needed coffee, while Todd just wanted to lay his head down on the table.

Eric, still new to making breakfast for multiple people, quickly recognized Marcie's look that said, "I need a cup of coffee, now, or I'll die."

Sighing in relief, Eric set down a steaming hot cup of French vanilla coffee. The smell alone made Marcie raise her head. She took a careful sip at first, then larger slurps, feeling life slowly returning to her body and, finally, her head. She glanced at Todd, who was still resting his head on the table. She smiled at him, took another sip, and then snapped upright.

"Eric," she whispered urgently.

With a pancake flipper in his hand, Eric leaned over, a curious look on his face. "What?" he whispered back.

"Todd told me last night that he can't do magic anymore!"

"What? He can't do magic anymore?" Eric asked, his voice rising in surprise.

Todd groaned and shifted in his chair at the table but seemed to have gone back to sleep.

"Eric, do you know what this means?" Marcie whispered, her voice filled with excitement.

"Yes, this is going to be such a relief for you—and well, for us," Eric whispered back, a smile creeping onto his face.

"We're going to be able to live normal lives again. I'm going to have a normal life!" Marcie's voice was getting louder, filled with joy.

"Yeah, it may be tough on Todd, but in the long run, it'll be good for him. He can go outside on his own, make friends, play sports . . . everything will open up for him!" Eric replied, his tone full of optimism.

Todd stirred and sat up. "I'm not hungry," he muttered. "I just want to go back to bed."

Marcie nodded. "That's fine. You can have something to eat when you're hungry," she said, her excitement hard to contain.

Todd slowly made his way back to his room and flopped down on his bed.

Back in the kitchen, Marcie asked, "If he can't do magic anymore, does that mean everything he did will be undone?"

Eric thought for a moment. "I don't think so. Nothing seems to have changed, right?"

Marcie smiled.

"I'm sure glad this happened after I was a dude again."

Back in Todd's room, he lay awake, feeling sullen. What was he going to do now that he couldn't do magic anymore? He turned the thought over in his mind until an idea sparked. He rolled over to his small nightstand, carefully pulled open the drawer, and retrieved a box. Gently, he opened it. Inside, nestled in a padded compartment, rested a golden ring. The engravings on it were unfamiliar to him, but they looked cool. He'd made the ring while creating the wedding rings, inspired by a design he'd read about in his book.

Todd lifted the ring out of the box and held it in his hand. It gleamed brightly in the soft light. As he slipped it onto his finger, he could feel it pulse with energy. A mischievous grin spread across his face.

This is going to be fun, he thought.